MJ MARSTENS
ANN DENTON

Le Rue Publishing
320 South Boston Avenue, Suite 1030
Tulsa, OK 74103
www.LeRuePublishing.com

ISBN: 978-1-951714-08-6

To All the Girls Who Wanna Get Hammered...

PRELUDE

KHEPRI

In the Earthly realm, there's a saying—*it's nothing personal*, but in the godly world, there's no such thing.

Everything is personal, and everything is done with an intent.

Take, for example, my job at the Black Hole Prison, or the *Back Hole* as the prisoners call it. Those prisoners specifically being demigods who have committed "godly crimes."

Nothing could have been more calculated than me taking one of the coveted positions as a prison guard.

Or, me currently undercover in scarab-form, buzzing through the trees outside the prison walls at the Back Hole, approaching a pile of shit.

Scarab is just a fancier name for *dung beetle*, but if the humans want to worship a shit-eater, who am I to stop them? I'm not just a crap god, either, I swear. I was one of the three most important solar deities in the Egyptian pantheon—*not that anyone recalls this.*

Forgive me if I sound bitter, not better, but fuck if it doesn't chap my ass that my duties were constantly overlooked for those of the almighty and popular Ra's. That fuckstick never even did half the work I did! As the god of the midday sun, Ra merely used to take the brilliant ball of fire from my hands and roll it leisurely to Atum, who was in charge of the evening, or setting sun.

But because Ra's sun shone the brightest and was at the zenith in the sky when humans were awake, they worshipped his golden ass most. Atum got a little more glory than me. His sunsets made him legendary.

But me?

I was the forgotten former sun god. When the sun set in the West, Atum handed it to me to roll through Duat, the Egyptian underworld.

Do humans think that shit is easy?! Of the three of us sun gods, I had the ball the most, all night and into the morning. But I got the least appreciation. My wings flutter extra fast in irritation as I approach the huge mound of shit, a bouquet of scents wafting from it and hitting my antennae. But even the scent doesn't distract me from the memories of my former life.

My old job as sun roller didn't even end there in the underworld. In the morning, when I shoved the burning hot sun onto the horizon in the East, did Ra move his lazy ass to meet me?

Nope.

The fucker slept in—*till like ten a.m.*! Only then did he take over, when everyone revered the intense heat and light of his sun.

Why don't humans appreciate subtlety? Where was the adoration for my sunrises? Why did humans always bemoan getting up at the crack of dawn? Didn't they notice the gorgeous streaks I tried to lace through the sky? Their eyes were supposed to be programmed to see more colors at dawn than dusk, because I helped them slowly adjust from dark to light. Didn't they realize what an asshole I could have been, just shoving that bright yellow light at them all at once?

I give an annoyed squeak as I fly through Duat; that sound is the best I can do to express my frustration while I'm in my insect form.

I might be angry at the humans, but Ra's egotistical ass went above and beyond to gain their attention. He wined and dined them, essentially, until Atum and I were forgotten.

We finally gave up and just let Ra have all the glory. *And all the work.*

If Ra wanted to be the main Egyptian solar deity, then he sure as Duat could have all the trappings that came with it. Atum and I said fuck it and let Ra have the fire ball full time.

Like I said, I'm bitter, *not better*, about it, but I'm not fucking enraged about him taking over. Certainly, not enough to want to exact revenge on Ra's narcissistic ass.

No, it was only when Ra started doing something *even worse than stealing all my glory and worship* that I was spurred into my current personal vendetta against the man.

Not only worse, *but evil.* The asshole's created a prison to lock up demigods. And he's throwing them in right and left.

Hence why I am in my scarab-form and flying straight into a fetid pile of shit. Said shit pile is none other than Nut, goddess of the cosmos, in disguise. *Clever goddess.* Who would suspect a mound of crap? And what better thing to attract a dung beetle, right? I land right on top of her, trying not to laugh.

"Wow. You went all out. You're still *steaming.*"

"It's cow manure," she comments, unfazed. Two eyes pop open in the shit and I'm caught staring at something that looks like a cross between the poop emoji on my phone and a hieroglyphic cartoon face.

The cow manure bit makes sense since Nut is also the goddess of cows. The question is—*did she literally shit herself out of her cow form for this?* The bigger question is—*do I want to really know?*

Not really.

"Impressive," I tease instead of asking my questions. "I guess I should have said something like 'holy cow' or 'holy shit.'"

"Always the joker, aren't you, my Khepri? I don't

relish being fecal matter, but for my son, I am happy to be dung all my life. How is he?"

"He is well. Hopeful and strong. He knows that we will free him. He sends his love." The Demigodling always asks me to tell his mother this, whether Ra has tortured him or not, which happens more often than not. He doesn't want her to worry. But Nut is very familiar with Ra's tactics, since the dickwad tried to prevent her from ever having children.

Nut doesn't say anything, but her cartoon eyes fill with tears. It's strange to talk to bodily waste. It's even stranger to see it cry.

"There, there, mother," I soothe. "You're turning into diarrhea. Pull yourself together."

Nut really isn't my mother. I'm a special deity in that I don't come from a parental meeting of a dick in a vag, (I created myself out of the fabric of the universe) but Nut is one of the few gods to acknowledge, and even care for me. Being even older than me, she's become a mother figure of sorts over the centuries. I love her dearly and would do anything for her—*even take on Ra.*

See, before I willed myself into existence—that's right, I'm also the god of reincarnation—I was born a scarab beetle from nothing but another glorious pile of poop.

But enough about me. Nut and I are on a mission to destroy the sun fuck and his awful unjust prison. I'm not the only one who hates Ra.

Nut and Ra have been at one another's throats for millennia—ever since she ticked him off and turned him down to marry Geb, the Earth god.[1] Ra was so jealous that he tried to prevent Nut from having children. When she outwitted him with Thoth's help, Ra tried to kill her offspring. He even went so far as to permanently separate Nut from Geb. So, Nut stooped —*per Ra's godist, biased opinion*—to sleeping with a human man and having a demigodling.[2]

If that wasn't offensive enough—the Egyptian people ignored Ra's wish to be their King Maker. The humans declared Nut's child god their pharaoh. The demigodling's worship stats soon surpassed Ra; enraging the sun god even further because he was left in the shadow of this spawn of fucking.

Except—*gods don't believe anything's an accident, right?*

Everything's personal to them and Ra took every move that Nut made as an audacious slight.

So, Ra, the deviant fuck, had to be crafty. He devised a way to frame the Demigodling. Ra made it appear as if the Demigodling attempted to kill his half-siblings for their power. As god of justice—*anyone else see the irony here*—Ra sentenced the Demigodling to jail, a.k.a: *a lifetime in a piece-of-crap holding in the depths of Duat, the Egyptian Underworld, called the Black Hole.*

Of course, the accusation was a pile of crap lies, and I know a thing or two about piles of shit.

Nut also knew it was bullshit, but her other children were not so sure. Ra, the fucker, offered irrefutable evidence of the Demigodling's guilt. Only Thoth supported the goddess of the Cosmos and her half-breed's innocence. *Oh, and me.* Having had a taste of Ra's ability to twist people's minds for his personal benefit (i.e. becoming the major sun god), shall we say, I already knew what the jerk was capable of.

So, I promised Nut that I would free her son.

I gave Ra all my solar power and have pretended to be his admiring lackey in exchange for a spot as head guard at the Back Hole—I mean *Black Hole*—though the prisoners inside are getting a dry-assed fucking.

Initially, the plan was to understand the layout and the holding of the jail and for Thoth to think of a plan to spring the Demigodling. Rules are different in Duat —*even for gods*, and Anubis, the god of the underworld, is buddy-buddy with Ra-Fuck, giving the sun god an advantage.

But, over time, Ra has been adding to his prison, adding extensive booby traps that constantly change, and adding prisoners faster than a seven-year-old girl adds sequins with a bedazzling gun.

And all of the prisoners are demigods.

Over time, I realized that Ra's true anger stems from her son being half-human, the breedist bastard.

"Ra's adding another demigod tonight. Dionysus' son," I tell Nut.

"Oh? And what has he *supposedly* done?"

"I think his crime is getting humans too drunk to properly worship their gods." I roll my eyes at the

trumped up charges that gods come up with to elimi-
nate their unwanted family members.

Nut snorts and bits of fecal matter splatter my face,
which I happily lick up.

Don't you fucking judge me. I'm a dung beetle. I
survive off of this shit. Literally.

"Ra's systematically adding all the half-breeds," Nut
breathes in horror.

"Yes, and he's almost done. I ... I worry about what
will happen when he has the last demigod secured."

"I must tell Thoth this. Maybe he can help hide
those who are left. We need to get my son out of there
before it is too late."

"I agree, Mother. I will work on finding the
elemental weaknesses of the holding and meet you
again in a week."

"Go in shit, my Khepri," she says in parting.

I laugh.

"I'm knee-deep in it every day where I work," I tell
her before flying off.

VAL

"DAD, I CAN'T COME OUT—*I HAVE CORONAVIRUS*!" I prevaricate through the thick wooden doors of my bedroom.

It's sad, *so sad*, that I'm a twenty-seven year old woman lying to her father, but here we are—*a step in the wrong direction of maturity*. But if it means getting out of dinner with my hateful stepmothers and condescending siblings, then, so be it. Stupid family traditions. Why do I torture myself with them?

Oh right. Because I actually love my dad.

I blow a raspberry as I stare at the wooden beams of my bedroom ceiling, which span thirty feet overhead.

I can literally hear my father facepalm in frustration through the door. How can I hear it? Because the god of storms is never quiet.

I roll sideways on my pure-white down comforter and stare at the door, wondering if he'll barge in.

"Sigrdrifa, gods *can't* become sick," my father, the almighty Thor, reminds me dryly.

"*Val*, Dad. I want to be called Val, remember? And I'm only half-god. The *human* part of me is sick." I fake cough loudly at the door. I catch myself doing so in the mirror and waggle my tongue at my reflection.

My blue eyes peer back at me and I try to wink one, then the other. My mirror looks tiny in this room. All of my furniture does, because even though it was built for a goddess, I'm pretty sure my dad assumed I'd grow wings one day like my sisters and want to fly around in my room.

Nope.

Wingless here.

Wingless and a shameless liar.

I'm being so immature. But I can't help it. Even though I love Dad, I also love to remind him what an utter sacrifice it is to attend these drawn out, Spanish Inquisition style meals.

Asgard dinners should come with a warning: Guard your ass in Asgard. Or you'll get fucked raw.

Now, my father groans in exasperation and there's a *thump*, like his forehead has just hit the door. "Daughter," he warns.

I clutch my stomach and give my mirror an Oscar-worthy performance as I croak, "I'm serious. It's bad, and until the godly CDC makes an announcement, I don't think we should risk it. I need to self-quarantine."

"Sigrdrifa!" my father booms, refusing to use my

chosen name. The plaster walls around me shake from the roar of his voice. "You will come to dinner or you will be on goat duty for a month!"

I make a face.

A month of cleaning goat shit?!

Well, I'm a grown woman. If I don't want to come to dinner, then I won't. I cross my arms and tell myself that.

Unfortunately, my father doesn't see twenty-seven as *grown*. In fact, compared to him, I'm still an infant —*which would explain why he treats me like one*. There's no point in telling him that in the human world, I'm an adult.

"My house, my rules," he thunders.

Literally.

My bedroom door starts to shake and a bit of cloud drifts under the door.

"Dad, you're clouding again," I tell him. I sigh. He used to make his clouds only as needed, but now that he's older, sometimes they pop out like unwanted ear hair.

"I'm only clouding because my youngest child is refusing to come to family dinner!" he yells.

His hand touches the doorknob and I can tell the second it happens because a lightning bolt shoots through the keyhole and zings across the room. If my peach curtains weren't fireproof, they'd be ablaze.

"Dad!" I scold as I slide off the bed and stand with my arms crossed when he slams my door open.

I see my father, red hair billowing in a wind of his own making[1] while his bearskin cape trails along the floor. He's shirtless. Ever since the Marvel movies came out, my father's gone shirtless, as if there's some kind of competition between him and Chris Hemsworth.[2] It's a little embarrassing, to be honest, but his worship rates have shot through the roof since then. Housewives everywhere chant his name as they come … and since my father is a god of fertility in addition to thunder, he's pretty damn smug about that shit.

"I will not have a child of mine—"

I parrot back his oft-said rant, "I will not have a father of mine—"

He freezes. "You mock me?"

"Yes."

"No one mocks me."

"To your face? No. They don't." Loki and I mock him behind his back all the time.

Dad's hammer is in his hand and he smacks it down against his open palm like a judge with a gavel. "One night! I ask for one night a week. If you loved me—"

"I do love you, you pompous ass! In spite of your powers!"

Dad's hammer freezes midswing. His bushy brows furrow. "What?"

"I said I love you," I sigh, the fight draining out of me as I pick at my wrinkled t-shirt.

"Not that part, the other part."

"In spite of your powers?" I ask, uncertainly.

Dad swoops forward and gives me a one armed hug, nearly crushing me. He kisses the top of my head. "That is the truest kind of love. I love you too, Val. Now, get dressed for dinner. I've got to go hide my hammer so your sisters don't try to take it again."

"Perhaps you should bring it with you. The time they tried to grab it was hilarious." None of my sisters can lift his hammer an inch. I can pick it up no problem.

My ancient father wags a finger at me. "No. I want no drama tonight. Now get dressed or prepare to clean out the barn!" He stomps off, slamming the door shut behind him. He's under the illusion that hiding his hammer actually works. I know every hiding spot he has. Under the pillow. Behind the huge painting of himself (at dick level and no, I don't want to consider the implications of that), or in the crowded umbrella stand. He's not all that creative.

After he leaves, I sink right back into making faces at the closed door, like the child that I'm *not*. I play *eenie meenie miney moe* to determine what I should do. Ultimately, I decide that sixty minutes of misery outranks thirty days of manure work for a couple of old, gassy goats.

"Fine," I yell as I hear Dad's footsteps retreat. Huffing, I drag myself out of bed and get dressed for this blessed "family" event.

Please note that I use the word *family* in the most scathing of terms possible.

What my dad has is not what I would call a 'family unit.'

It's more like a dysfunctional gathering of gods that my father either slept with or spawned. I'm one of the spawn, obviously. The lowliest of his children because I'm, *gasp*, half-human. As if this is *my* fault, but my obnoxious siblings and their disdainful mothers can't scorn Thor—*at least not openly*, so they turn their rancor on me.

A bunch of charmers, that group.

And lucky me, I get to go eat with them. That's exactly what I want to do on my vacation from Earth and my job at Home Depot. I want to spend my work-free time listening to people who hate me.

I quickly pull on a pair of faded, torn jeans and an *Animaniacs* T-shirt sporting the Brain and his bid for world domination. I freaking love that mouse. How Mickey remains more popular, I'll never know.

I hum the cartoon's theme song as I toss my long brown hair up into a ponytail and debate adding makeup, but what good is it when I'm competing with gods? The jerkwads can make their skin *glitter*, for crying out loud—*I forego the mascara*. Then, I grace-lessly stomp down the long corridor to the main floor and into the opulent dining room.

The room itself is massive. It's full of carved wooden beams detailing ships and dolphins, islands and massive waves that stretch across the ceiling. The walls are covered in obnoxious paintings of my relatives, which my eyes studiously avoid. I make my way to an eighty-foot-long table. Everything on it from the silverware to the bowls is made of gold.

I'm greeted by the sight of two elegant women dressed to the nines in sparkling dresses and a gaggle of my siblings, most decked out in their battle gear.

I spot my least favorite sister already seated, blonde head tipped back as she chugs some mead. Leaned against her chair is her weapon. If Skeggjöld[3] can bring her ax to dinner, then I can bring my cell to text Dev, my *human* BFF.

How the man got my phone to work in Asgard is mind-blowing, but Devin is a tech wizard. He's also smarter than any god that I've ever met—*not* that I'm ever going to admit that out loud to anyone, especially Dev. That's a good way to place a target on his head if the gods knew. Or make his head swell, if *he* knew, not that Devin is conceited, by any means. Even though he's hot, he's one of the most down-to-earth people that I know. Humble, but knows his strengths.

I bite down on a smile as I picture his reddish-brown hair, beard, and goofy grin. I couldn't ask for a better best friend, but everyone else here tonight would most assuredly disagree.

Bunch of superior beings.

I personally feel that they can choke on a dick and mind their own business. I don't tell them how to do their god stuff; they can butt out of my human affairs.

Of course, this is just wishful thinking on my part. What god can resist torturing humans?

No sooner do I sit down, than do my glorious step moms begin their weekly rant. (Yes. Step *moms*. Double the nitpicking. Double the fun.)

"Ugh. Sigrdrifa, what are you wearing?! It's positively putrid," Sif, the goddess of *family*, sneers at me, looking down her long, hooked nose. Apparently, she hasn't kept up with the times and realized that tiny button noses are in, but I'm not about to tell her this.

Járnsaxa, my father's other consort, giggles next to her like a schoolgirl. Her blonde curls and giant breasts bounce in tandem as she giggles.

Really mature, ladies.

Of course, with my father out of the room, they feel safe, emboldened even, to verbally attack me. But, because I'm classy, I don't say anything.

At first.

"Yes," one of my many sisters adds, "you're a disgrace to the Valkyrie name! Frankly, I'm surprised that your fashion sense hasn't landed you in the half-breed jail. The Black Hole seems like the perfect place for a weirdo who loves human eccentricities. I mean, look at those pants you're wearing. They're torn to shreds! Were you in a bar fight with a cat? Did you lose? Don't even get me started on your shirt."

Everyone laughs.

My step moms laugh.

My sisters laugh.

My brothers laugh.

I laugh.

Ha, ha, ha ...

I clear my throat dramatically before responding.

"Me, going to jail, because I lack *your* fashion sense. Brilliant. And a bar fight with a cat. That's funny, Skeggjöld. Good ones. *Alas*, my pants really got torn when your boyfriend tried to rip them off of me in a fit of passion. Not the brightest bulb, that guy. I told him to use the button and the zipper, but I guess he's just used to the ease of skirts and *even easier* women. Did I mention that I like yours? Skirt, that is. Are those leather strips? Super fucking tasteful. I'm so glad that you can escape the Black Hole because of your full-goddess status, because you sure wouldn't be smart enough to escape otherwise." I end with a smile.

On the outside, I'm a smug little brat, but on the inside, I'm seething. *Could I make it five minutes without one of my dick siblings or their dick moms ragging on my heritage?* I'm half-human—*an abomination*, apparently—I get it, as if being magicless wasn't reminder enough.

I just smile sweetly and wait for the explosion.

It doesn't take long. Half a second passes before Skeggjöld, whom I've secretly nicknamed *Skanky*, is launching herself across the table, her battle ax raised above her head.

The step moms squawk indignantly and my other siblings join the argument. It's a blond mob against me, but I'm smarter than *all* of them. I timed my barb

9

perfectly and my father enters the fray just as my darling sister is about to split my skull. Immediately, he throws up a hand and freezes time for everyone but me.

He marches over and plucks the ax out of my blonde sister's hand where it's just about to shave my ear from my head. He tosses the ax on the floor.

I take a moment to appreciate the unattractive scrunch of my stepmothers' noses. I kind of hope Dad notices it. I mean, it's rare to catch a god looking so shitty. Part of me wants to lift my phone and see if I can take a picture and text it to Devin. But that won't go over well. My friend, Asteio, told me about a demigod whose mother tried to have him jailed for sending out photos of her without a glowing aura. I can only imagine the consequences for truly embarrassing photographs.

I glance over at Dad, who's rubbing his red beard and shaking his head as he looks at me.

"Sigrdrifa, what have you done now?" Dad asks wearily.

"Father," I huff in pretend outrage and toss a hand on my chest, "you wound me! Why is it always my fault? You know I didn't start it."

The mighty Thor sits down at the head of the table and rests his head on his palm. He stares at me with the worn-out affection of bedraggled parents everywhere. That shit doesn't go any different for humans or gods, at least not in my experience.

"I know, my daughter, but I am sick of ending it. Is it too much to ask for everyone to get along?"

I snort.

"It is for your other wives and their kids. You know me well enough. If they treated me decently, I'd be happy to reciprocate. Instead, they treat me like trash and I refuse, absolutely refuse, to let them continue," I hiss in a fierce whisper. I was raised in Asgard after my mom died, but since I've been living more on Earth, I've learned about a lot of things. Like human rights. And dignity.

My dad smiles sadly.

"You're so much like your mother," he comments, surprising me by talking about her.

My mother was the love of his life, even though she was human. She passed away twenty years ago. We never speak of it, but I'm fairly certain that she didn't die by normal, human means. Personally, I think one of my step moms had her killed, but that's just conjecture on my part. Dev and I have searched for clues, but there's nothing amiss in her human obit and no autopsy was done. That, coupled with the fact that my father refuses to talk about her passing, gives me zero cause to think that she was murdered, but I can feel it in my gut.

A Valkyrie knows when death is natural or not. And even though I'm only part Valkyrie, with no actual powers, I still feel a twinge. Like the time this customer tried to steal a saw at Home Depot by stuffing it under his shirt and I told him one day he'd end up cutting his own dick off for being that stupid … who did I see in the paper the next week? *Dead? With his dick cut off?* Front page stuff.

So, while I don't have powers, I have *inklings*.

"Val," Dad begins, surprising me by using my chosen name, "you know that I think you're wonderful, right?"

"Ugh—getting mushy on me already?" I tease, but I soften at his tone. Unlike a lot of gods, he doesn't shun me or any other demigods. Under it all, my father is truly a great guy. "I know. I just get … tired of all of this. It hurts, Dad," I confess in embarrassment.

Valkyries don't talk about their emotions—*or admit to having weaknesses*.

"I'm sorry, daughter. I know it doesn't seem like it, but I'm always in your corner, fighting for you; however, I can't outwardly show favoritism."

"So, you're admitting I'm your favorite?" I perk up a little.

Dad lets out one more sigh and shakes his head fondly. "I don't have favorites." He winks and then releases his hold on time.

Everyone unfreezes and movement begins again. Instantly, Skanky is rushing toward me, but my father raises a hand and lightning arcs across the table and into my sister, who immediately goes down. She lays there, twitching for a few seconds, until she recovers.

It's a brilliant couple of seconds.

Immediately upon recovery, Skeggjöld scrambles

back to her seat, bowing her blonde head meekly.

"One dinner!" Dad shouts, "One dinner, once a week—*is that too much to ask for?!* No one in this room is a child. For Mjölnir's[4] sake, my goats are better behaved."

I make a face at the mention of his beloved Tanngrisnir and Tanngnjóstr, the two goats who pull my dad's chariot. Dad loves them, but I spent enough time in my childhood herding the little shits to never wanna see them again. Tanngrisnir is okay, your typical smelly eternal goat and all. But Tanngnjóstr? She's a kinky jerkwad who likes to try to chew on my panties *while I'm still wearing them!* No wonder her name means 'teeth grinder.'

Dad's voice amps up, like he's raring for battle. "I am *done*. From this moment on, if no one can behave civilly, they are not welcome in my house or on my land. They are undeserving. Am I understood?"

Everyone stares at him in horror.

Thor basically just said that, in addition to disowning their selfish asses, he would strip them of their powers. I cover my mouth to hide my smug grin. This threat isn't for me—*I don't have any powers.*

No favorites, my ass.

While his declaration weighs the rest of them down, I'm not bothered at all. I certainly don't care about his home or land. Dad knows that I would much prefer to live in the human realm than in Asgard, but he guilts me into staying one night a week because I'm his only link to mom. Nope, this threat is for everyone else because they are practically useless, even with their powers. Gods are used to having someone cater to their every whim, whereas I prefer to do shit myself. My siblings and step moms wouldn't last a day without Thor's generosity.

Or their powers.

Because among the gods, power is what defines you.

Another reason that I'm persona non grata.

I'm powerless and half-human.

After several seconds of tense silence, my father raises his hand for the servers to bring the food and we eat, golden utensils clinking softly in the uncomfortable silence. The rest of dinner is fairly uneventful, but I take the opportunity to chew with my mouth open when looking at my step moms.

Childish?

Absolutely.

Watching them nearly barf at the sight of my half-masticated Gellur[5]?

Fucking priceless.

When dessert is whisked off the table, I rush over to Dad and kiss his cheek. Then, I run from the room before he can command me to stay. I need to escape. I need normalcy. Friendship. Kindness. Laughter and fun.

I need to connect with my humanity once more.

I need Dev.

2

DEV

I CLICK DONE ON A PROJECT THAT HAS NOTHING TO DO with work—a project that could get me in a shitload of trouble if anyone ever found out, but it's worth it.

Then I send off a text: **Project complete. Awaiting payment.**

The responding text is a single emoji: *a heart*.

I narrow my eyes. If that jerkwad is gonna try and cheat me ... well, there's nothing I can do about it. You don't fuck with a demigod—any god, really. That's how you end up deader than the Wicked Witch of the East. Getting crushed by houses isn't really on my kick-the-bucket list.

Luckily, a second text comes through a minute later: **Payment on its way.**

'On its way.'

What does that mean? I wonder.

I lean back in my company-issued desk chair and

swivel side to side, trying to figure out how payment could be on its way so soon.

Doesn't magic take awhile?

But seconds later, I hear a tap at the window outside my office. I turn to see a little cherub floating there in midair. He's got the stereotypical blond curls, but he is sporting a leather jacket with a spike-studded collar and sunglasses.

"Hurry the fuck up," the floating baby curses profanely at me.

My eyes widen as I stand and walk across my narrow office to undo the latch and slide the window open. The cheap thing is worse than my chair and sticks—I have a little trouble getting the damn window to open. For a second, I have flashbacks of working at a fast food drive thru as a teen.

And those are never cheerful memories.

The baby cupid rests a chubby elbow on the windowsill, letting his jacket gape open over his bare chest, then he shoves his glasses up. I can't help but notice he still has on the traditional loincloth under-neath the leather jacket. It totally looks like a diaper, just like the pictures.

"So … the website's ruined?" he asks.

I force myself to focus on his face and stop wondering about how comfortable—*or uncomfortable*—that loincloth is. Did he use it like a diaper?!

"It's still running. But I did exactly as Aeneus[1] requested. All the matchmaking software has been corrupted. Aphrodite and Eros will have a huge mess trying to sort out unhappy, mismatched couples."

The cupid[2] gets an evil grin.

"Boss man's gonna like that shit. His mom pissed him off big time."

I nod, not quite sure what to do with my hands. I scratch my beard for a second but, then, decide that it makes me look nervous, so I slide them into my pockets.

"As I said—job's done. I'd like my payment."

"Bet you would." The little cupid reaches a dimpled hand behind his back into what looks like midair. But it must be his invisible quiver because he comes back with an arrow.

He hands it over to me.

"Remember, these babies are a one-time use thing. Only a god can reverse the effects. I know you moderns don't use bows and arrows. So, just prick the lucky girl or guy with it, and then you can *prick* them, you feel me?"

I nod, ignoring his uncouth words. All my attention is on the love arrow in my hands. It's made of many different materials—wood with some ivory-looking inlay, and is delicately and intricately carved—like the lace on a Valentine. *I can't believe I'm holding one.* I balance it gently on my palms like it's a museum arti-fact. Which, I suppose, it would be, if other humans knew the gods existed.

But they don't.

Cupid clicks his tongue and gives me some finger guns. "Nice doing business with you." Then he flies off, leaving me frozen, still standing in front of my window.

I study the stone arrowhead, the carved wooden shaft, the pink feathers on the back edge.

I swallow hard.

Maybe ... maybe one day ... I'll have the guts to use this, I tell myself. *I just need the right moment.*

Just then, someone knocks at the door—most likely my boss. *Dammit!* I shove my window shut—thankfully, the damn thing doesn't stick this time. Then, I run over and put the arrow into my desk drawer and slam it closed, heart pounding as I pull up a new screen on my computer.

Code flashes across the screen for the very mundane, human healthcare billing project I'm supposed to be tweaking.

"Come in!" I call, even though my palms are sweaty and my heart rate is out of control. The sooner I let the boss in, the sooner he'll be gone.

Sure enough, the door opens and there stands Mr. Roberts. I feel like the guy from *Office Space*, trying to avoid getting wrangled into working on the weekend. I resolutely stare at my boss' tie while he talks.

After five minutes of mindless chatter and check-ins, he leaves and I can breathe again—*I guess he didn't want me to come in on Saturday.* I turn back to my computer and start on a project that he wants done.

I crack open a soda and take a sip before diving headfirst into the world of *Ruby on Rails* and lines of code that sing like music.

My phone rings and startles me so badly that I knock over my soda with my elbow and completely soak my robin's egg blue pants—which is bad because that's where my phone is, but at least it's not my work computer.

"Shit!" I say as I try to rescue my phone from the cold, sticky mess.

"Whoa, sorry. Is this a bad time? I can call back later."

I hear Val's lilting voice with that soft elusive accent and immediately freeze. *Wait. What's happening?* I glance at the phone in my hand like an idiot. *Shit.* I accidentally answered it. I hold the dripping thing up to my ear.

"Hello?"

"Dev?"

Val's voice is like a shot of whiskey. It makes my throat burn and I get light-headed.

Every.

Single.

Damn.

Time.

"Hey."

I ignore the soda that's now dripping into my eardrum. I can deal with that later. I know that Val's at her dad's. So, if she's calling, it must be serious.

19

"What's up?"

"I want to tie up my stepmothers and launch them into another plane of existence where they have to hear their own nasally voices echoing back at them for eternity."

"So, it was a good family dinner then?" I joke, grinning.

She's so dramatic, my Val.

"The best."

"Come back to Earth and I'll give you a make-up dinner."

The words are out of my mouth before I can really think them through. As soon as I say them, my throat grows tight. It almost sounded like I asked for a date. *Will Val think it's a date?* I scrub a hand over the back of my neck. I might puke. *What if she thinks it's a date and says no?*

"A make-up family dinner?" Val wonders. I can picture her face. She's probably chewing on her bottom lip.

My stomach drops and my chest lightens at the same time. I'm both disappointed and relieved at her interpretation of dinner as a platonic thing.

"Yeah," I grit out, trying not to let my voice get pitchy.

I clear my throat and bat down the self-loathing that smacks me across the face and makes my cheeks burn.

"I'll have to sneak out ... one second."

I hear a scraping sound and, then, the crunch of leaves underfoot.

"What are you doing?" I ask.

"Shhh," she shushes me, like anyone else could hear our conversation.

For all I know, maybe the gods in Asgard can. She's never told me about anyone with that kind of power, but her family is huge. *Who knows?*

Val is the first demigod I've ever met. I remember that day perfectly. I'd come in for my night shift at Home Depot, my college job of stocking shelves—*which far surpassed my high school job of fast-food bitch.* There Val stood, on the loading dock, dark brown hair billowing in the wind like she was on a magazine cover, plush lips pursed with attitude, and a tattoo of a woman on her forearm that told me Val loved hard, deep, and permanently.

I immediately fell for her.

I was shocked that first night when we had to do team carries and she chose me as her partner. I'd been delighted when I'd made her laugh and startled when she'd shown me that she didn't actually need help carrying a hundred pound box.

My eyes had gotten as big as balloons. At first, I'd thought she was just like a bodybuilder or something.

But a month later, she'd confessed she was a demigod in the employee kitchen while we were on a Ding Dong break at two a.m.

ANN DENTON & MJ MARSTENS

"You're joking." I'd paused with a mouth full of chocolate cake and lips coated with white filling.

Val had pressed her gorgeous lips together and set down her Ding Dong. Then she'd grabbed her phone and dialed.

Three seconds later ... I'd nearly died of a heart attack. Because a dude with a Grateful Dead t-shirt and grey goat legs appeared in the break room. Out of nowhere.

I'd tried to shove Val behind me—do the protector thing while I tried to figure out if I was being punked, if this dude was a magician, or if my Ding Dongs had been spiked with LSD.

But Val had only laughed and pushed me aside. "Dev, this is Asteio. He's another demigod. He's got actual powers, unlike me. Asteio, would you mind showing Dev?"

Asteio had waved his hand and, immediately, his goat legs had turned human. Unfortunately, that had meant the rest of his lower body turned human too— including his dick, which was hanging out because he hadn't worn pants.

"Whoa! I meant your other powers!" Val had given a girlish giggle that I'd never heard before. A flirtatious giggle that made me feel like grabbing the microwave off the countertop and hurling it at Asteio.

I hadn't.

But I'd wanted to. And I'd never been a very violent guy before that.

Asteio had put back his goat legs then wiggled his fingers and shot wine through the air like a stream from a water fountain. I'd been so shocked I hadn't opened my mouth and the wine had hit me in the face, soaked my shirt, and gotten me fired after our shift manager had appeared and Asteio had magically disappeared at the same time.

The shift manager hadn't believed my story about a magic goat man shooting wine at me. Go figure.

Val had walked me out. "I'm so sorry. That wasn't fair." The shift manager hadn't listened to Val argue. He hadn't fired her, because, well, before *her* the only woman on the night shift had been a middle-aged bruiser named Mandi.

"Life's not fair," I'd tried to shrug it off and focus on more important things. Like the fact that deities actually existed. And procreated with humans. And semi deities might do the same. "So, you really are a half god?"

She'd gotten this adorable blush. "Yeah."

"Do ... you mind me asking which god?"

She'd glanced around nervously. "Can I tell you tomorrow?"

"You wanna see me tomorrow?"

"Can I stop by after work?"

My heart and dick remembered that moment in exact detail. The look on her face. This shy, sweet glance just for me. The tip of her teeth biting down on her lower lip.

23

"I want to get a taste of human life," she'd said.

I'd stepped forward, drawn in like a magnet, breath fleeing my lungs.

But then ... she'd friend-zoned me. She'd reached out and given me the arm pat of death. Not an arm brush. Not a suggestive touch. The old "buddy" arm pat.

And that's when I'd realized, she only thought of me as a friend.

Still only thinks of me as a friend.

I pull open my desk drawer and stare at the arrow. It looks so innocuous. So normal. It doesn't sparkle or glow or show any sign of magic. But ... it could make her mine.

Val.

My Val.

She could actually become *my* Val.

The bleating of goats through the phone brings me back to our conversation.

"What are you doing?" I ask.

"Hitching a ride," Val whispers. "Meet you on your rooftop in two hours."

I swallow hard. "Yup, sounds good."

Two hours. Shit. That doesn't give me much time. I snatch up the arrow and hang up the phone. I march out of the office before seven p.m. for once.

Because Val and I have a date.

A dinner.

With destiny.

3

VAL

I'M REALLY GRATEFUL FOR CLOUD COVER SINCE I DIDN'T think to grab any of Dad's stored bags of clouds from the stable before I left. It would have been really awkward to have to explain flying a cart driven by goats through the sky.

If Dad had reindeer, no one would bat an eyelash to see them flying. Humans would think it was some publicity stunt for Christmas.

But goats?

Nobody remembers anymore that Thor brings the thunder by driving his goat-led cart through the clouds. That's one of the things Dad constantly bemoans when I visit, because Chris Kringle makes a killing off of reindeer merch. But a red-nosed American Pygmy on a shirt just gets you weird looks. I know. I tried it.

Luckily, I don't have to come up with some half-assed explanation for my actions because nobody sees me before I land on Dev's roof.

I clamber out ungracefully, my human side rearing its klutzy head, and toss the goats a couple of my old t-shirts to chew on before I head to the emergency stair-well. The shirts are a crappy snack but they were the best bribe I had in my room.

The stairwell door opens as I reach it and Dev steps out. He always has perfect timing. Sometimes, I feel like we have this strange psychic connection—*like he just knows what I'm thinking.*

It's crazy—certainly, all my sisters and my step-mothers tell me it is. *'Guys are idiots,'* they say, *'Guys don't understand anything.'*

But Dev gets me.

Like now, when he shows up carrying a dozen pink roses. My heart swells; he's the sweetest thing. I rush up to him and grab them.

"Oh, you're a lifesaver!" I exclaim and take the fragrant blooms from him. "The girls are starving after our trip."

I run back to Tanny and Tangy and hold out half the roses to each of them. Their bulging little caprine eyes light up as they both chomp down on a perfect rose. Their bleats of pleasure make my heart soar.

I spent a lot of time with these hircin beauties growing up in Asgard, and roses are their favorite. Dev's never even met them before, but he must have looked up goat foods before I got here.

He's so thoughtful like that.

Dev comes up to stand beside me.

"You're amazing," I compliment and give him a hip bump. Ecstasy zips through me, just like it does every time I touch him—*which isn't often.*

I glance up at him, to see if I have the same effect on him that he has on me but he doesn't look exactly happy, let alone ecstatic. His face is strained and his lips pursed together tightly.

"Glad I made someone's night," he mumbles as he bends forward stiffly to pet Tangy's head.

"Careful!" I laugh, grabbing his hand and pulling it back as Tangy bares her teeth at him. "Not nice," I scold the goat, who rolls her eyes at me.

I get attitude from an animal that would eat used condoms.

Typical.

I drop the rest of the roses onto the roof so that the animals can finish their treat, and I head inside with Dev.

He doesn't drop my hand.

Does that mean he wants to hold it?

Touching him gives me the craziest thrill. My chest puffs full of air and anticipation, just like it does before my dad and I run through a lightning bolt obstacle course that he's made on the outskirts of Asgard. Dev's touch is as potent as the fear of getting struck by lighting.

Part of me wants to squeeze Dev's hand to let him

27

know how I feel, but Dev's human, and I'm not entirely sure if it would hurt him or not. Once, I accidentally crushed a brick in my hand. I didn't realize how fragile they were, and *humans are way more breakable*. I don't know the correct pressure ratio for human-hand squeezing to ensure that I don't hurt Dev.

He's just so adorable. I love how the tips of his ears turn pink all the time. I have no idea why they do that. Most humans' ears don't seem to change color as often as his. Other people's ears change if they are too cold or too hot, but Dev's seem to constantly be the delicate shade of the roses he brought for the girls.

And, let's not forget his grin—Dev's got this cute shy smile that makes me simultaneously melt and want to taste him to see if he's as sweet as he looks.

"Ready to go in?" Dev asks, interrupting my internal babbling as he scratches his beard with his free hand.

I lick my lips unconsciously. His brown eyes track their movement and the air is suddenly thick with something that I can't pinpoint.

"S-s-sure," I manage to stutter before collecting myself. "What kind of dinner are we having?"

"It's a surprise," he murmurs and my body tingles in awareness just like it does when someone uses magic nearby. Vibrations run underneath my skin.

Dev's voice is a little husky, and he drops my hand to hold open the door to the building for me. I go through first but wait to follow him down the semi-dark stairwell, since he knows it better than I do.

At one point I trip and grab onto Dev for balance. My breath catches. His shirt is so soft under my fingertips. I run my fingers over his back, tracing the line of his spine for a second before I realize what I'm doing.

I blink and step back. "Sorry." I can't believe I just touched Dev without invitation. Home Depot was incredibly clear about the rules for human interaction. Touching humans without their explicit permission and invitation is sexual harassment. People hate it.

That's why I try so hard not to touch him.

But sometimes, when I look at Dev, I just get so swept up in emotion that I forget. I'm uncertain if that's the deity in me—the god-like propensity to see something, want it, claim it—or if it's something else.

In either case, I know humans abhor it. I can count on one hand the number of times I've accidentally touched Dev. The first time I touched him was the time I told him I was a part-god, the night I'd nearly yanked his shirt and dragged him down on top of me so we could enjoy carnal bliss under the stars in the parking lot of Home Depot.

I hadn't had as much control over myself then. Or as much understanding of human ways, since Dad had basically raised me to tend his goats in Asgard. But I'd managed to restrain myself. I'd stopped. I'd uncurled my fingers and given him a gentle pat, backing away before the eternal, carnal part of me could debase and devalue him. I do the same now, backing up an entire step and holding up my palms in

ANN DENTON & MJ MARSTENS

surrender. "I'm so, so sorry, Dev. I fell. I didn't mean
to ..."

His cheeks heat. He must hate that I touched him
like that. But he's too embarrassed to say.

My Dev's always been easily embarrassed. He's shy.
It's one of my favorite things about him. Only humans
are shy. Gods are so entitled, they think everyone
wants to know their life story. They get offended when
someone hasn't already heard of them.

Gods are ridiculous.

Except for Dad. He's mostly okay I guess. Especially
when he's not surrounded by assholes. But most of the
time, he lives in the middle of that sewage pit he calls
family, breathing in their shit day in and day out until
his nose is immune to the stench. Kind of like the
people in Dalhart, Texas.

Dev's from there. He's told me about them. *Cow
Town*. The very air smells like cow patties. You can
taste it on your tongue. He's never wanted to go back.

I turn to focus back on Dev, who's already halfway
down the stairs. I grab the hand rail and hurry to catch
up, holding on tight so that if I fall, I'll at least face
plant into the wall instead of accidentally assaulting
Dev again.

I can't help but eye his ass once I've caught up
though. Even though he's a total computer nerd since
he left the Depot, he always goes to the gym. Five a.m.
like clockwork.

I'm not a stalker.

Not completely.

Only sometimes.

Fine. I am.

But shut up. I'm just looking, not touching.

And the Depot didn't say anything about looking. Gods watch humans all the time. And I'm part god. I can resist some impulses. But not all. *Not all.* Not when it comes to Dev.

He unlocks his apartment door and gestures for me to go in first. When I walk in, I stop short.

The lights are dimmed. There are candles lit on his dual purpose gaming and dining table. He's set out real silverware and plates. (We normally only use paper plates at his place because he doesn't have a dishwasher.) There's champagne chilling in a popcorn bucket full of ice. Two beer glasses stand next to it. His marijuana plants—his pride and joy—are nowhere to be found.

Hope fizzes in my belly, turning all my insides a bright frothy, exciting purple. It's like Dev has set off a bath bomb inside me. Those are my favorite human creations of all time. Their fizz and sizzle and purposelessness enchant me. I turn and look up at him, my throat suddenly tight and nervous. "What are we celebrating?"

Dev's face goes red and his hands fiddle inside his pockets. Something long, hard, and ... my excitement drops ... *thin*, presses against his jeans. No. No way. That's *too* thin. Relief floods me. No way that's a tiny cock. It's gotta be a pencil. Dev's playing with a pencil in his pocket. A sharp one based on the pointed tip.

He opens his mouth to speak, but just then my phone rings.

My phone only rings for emergencies.

Everyone literally only ever texts me.

I hold up a single finger and grab my phone out of my back pocket. "Hello?"

"Val?" a male voice on the cusp of crying calls out.

"Asteio!" I gasp. Son of Dionysus and a human, Asteio has been my friend since we were in nappies. He's the one who helped me prove gods exist to Dev. He's a half-goat man, possibly part of why we get along, because I know goats; he's also a very understanding shoulder to cry on.

"Val! I've been arrested!"

4

RAIDEN

FOR THE FIFTH TIME, I CIRCLE THE JAIL GROUNDS, searching for the ass-kisser who worships our boss, Ra. The last four times, the little brown-noser wasn't at his post. What the hell? I round the corner to find that Khepri has finally returned to his station.

"Where were you?" I boom in a thunderous voice.

The Egyptian god barely spares me a look as he fiddles with his golden arm bracelet. He's so arrogant, does he think he's that far above me? I want to punch him in his perfect nose and bruise his face until his blue eyes are swollen shut.

"Ra asked me to do something for him. Something *special*," he taunts.

I feel my lips twist into a grimace and lightning crackles under my skin. As the Japanese god of thunder, lightning, and storms, I control the weather. My people worship me to bring rain for crops. I am a fair

33

god, but I have very little patience for humans and their foolish ways. I can stave off drought, but anger me, and I will drown you in a monsoon. Every time I interact with Khepri, this stupid asshole who gave up being a sun god in order to be a pathetic God of Shit, I want to start a hurricane.

Why does this shithead get to be head guard?

"*Special?*" I sneer. "I knew it. You're sucking Ra's cock, huh? At least I can pride myself on doing honest work."

I've been searching for this asshole for the last hour so I can report the news. But does this fucker care about protocol? No ... he just slinks off. That's the third time this month he hasn't been at his post. And though I added extra areas to my rounds this afternoon, looking for him, I didn't see him. Suspicious.

Khepri snorts.

"Mommy and daddy got you this job— *don't delude yourself and your self-righteous sense of honesty.* As for what Ra wanted, that's none of your fucking business. It just makes you sound like a jealous little bitch. Besides, *you* don't get to question the head guard. Now, back to your post."

My eyes narrow into slits.

Every damn word out of this man's mouth is a lie; I can feel it in my bones, but the smug fuck is careful to cover his tracks. He truly is Ra's 'Golden Boy,' and, until I have irrefutable evidence that he's doing something shady when he sneaks off, I have to follow his orders. But, eventually, Khepri will fuck up and when he does, I'll be waiting to nail his ass to his ankh. That will be a glorious day. I'll have an artist make a sculpture of his humiliation so it can sit in a museum and stupid humans can ponder it for a thousand years.

I turn to do as 'ordered,' but call out nonchalantly, "I had to secure a new prisoner without your help. Son of Dionysis. He's been placed with the Demigodling for disrupting the peace and intoxicating the other prisoners."

This gets an immediate reaction from Khepri as I knew it would—*I fucking knew it.* The Egyptian god has an unnatural fascination with the Child God. The boy is no longer a kid, but it's what Ra calls him, other than Demigodling. The boss-man refuses to call the half-human by his given name—*nor should he.* Names are a privilege and anyone in this prison doesn't have a right to one. They're nothing but animals who have tried to tarnish the honorable names of the gods.

"Ra placed someone with the Demigodling?" Khepri asks incredulously, dropping his superior act for a second.

I raise a sardonic brow. "Didn't Ra tell you? Or was he too busy stuffing his dick down your throat to remember?"

Khepri's face turns red with anger and I feel supremely satisfied to have gotten under his skin. He might act like the poster guard of the year, but he's more rancid than curdled hippo milk. And I plan to expose him.

Actually, I plan on massacring him—*figuratively*.

When I finally discover the truth about Khepri's mysterious disappearances and reveal his secret to Ra, the insect deity can kiss his posh existence good-bye. And I can embrace my new position as head guard. It galls me to admit that my parents *did* pull some strings to get me this position at the Black Hole—a specialty prison for half-breeds who have committed heinous crimes against the gods.

Izanami and Izanagi are two of the most important primordial deities in the Shinto pantheon and, as such, I must live up to and serve our prestigious family name. By working at the Black Hole, I am helping to ensure that these prisoners are contained properly so that they cannot harm more gods. As such, this job is an honor and a service to protect my family from demigods. It would seem that their half-human nature makes them unstable and irrational in their conduct toward the divine.

In fact, it's my personal belief—and Ra's—that these prisoners are part of a network outside of the Black Hole that is specifically targeting major gods and goddesses. These traitorous fucks want to kill us all, but can't *if we can get to them first*.

"Raiden-Sama!" Khepri snaps, bringing my attention back to the present.

He stomps over to stand toe-to-toe with me. Another thing that galls me—Khepri is taller. Only by an inch or so, but he seems to use this to his advantage.

He has the typical Egyptian looks, but his skin is a deep chocolate brown and he wears his dark hair bluntly against his head. His eyes have a bright blue hue that is accented by the kohl that rims them. I've never seen an Egyptian god or goddess without their eye make-up, making me wonder if they draw it on every day or if it's literally a part of their skin.

In contrast, my skin is many shades lighter, but still very tanned. My hair is just as black, but I grow it long and wear it in the traditional warrior bun of my people. My eyes don't need any kohl to enhance them — their almond slant is another unique feature of my heritage. My shoulders are broader than Khepri's and I am much more muscled, a fact I know the female prisoners all appreciate. The catcalls when I do my rounds are enough to let a lesser god believe it's worship, some of the other guards do think it's worship. I let those fools look and admire all they want, but they can't touch. So, while Khepri is tall, I'm positive that I could kick his ass and win easily—*something I hope to eventually prove.*

"I told you to go back to your post. *Now!*" Khepri growls.

He whirls around and marches off in the direction of the Demigodling and the new inmate's cell. The Egyptian god's preoccupation with the Child God borders on fanaticism. As he walks away, I catch the stench of shit wafting from him.

"Ugh—did you leave the jail to go roll in shit? Is that your secret—*you have a crap fetish?*"

Maybe I was wrong about the cock sucking … maybe his mouth was kissing Ra's ass instead.

Who knows? He's a dung beetle after all.

Khepri freezes, his shoulders tense. The air between us is thick enough to cut with my katana. Just as suddenly, Khepri relaxes and even lets out a chuckle.

"You caught me," he drawls humorously. "I just *love* scat-play, but we all have our own little fucked-up secrets, don't we, Rai-Rai?"

He didn't!

This time, I don't try to stop him when he walks away because I'm too busy holding myself back as my face contorts. I'm a whole new level of pissed-off. The nickname alone would set me off, but for this bastard to insinuate that *I* have a secret is fucking unspeakable.

I am honorable.

I am godly.

I *am* Raiden-Sama.

And Khepri is a piece of shit that I am going to decimate.

5

VAL

I'M BACK AT THE MOST ABHORRENT EVENT KNOWN TO demigod-kind—*family dinner.*

Dad has also invited a couple of snooty Greek gods over this week. Something about Aphrodite being down about the lack of human love matches or some kind of bullcrap. He just wants in her skirts. *Everyone* wants in her skirts—even *I* watch her ass when she walks out of a room and I am strictly interested only in the D.

a.k.a Dev.

The only saving grace for this dinner is that I plan to use it to my advantage. I plan to commit a crime the gods find so heinous, they'll throw my ass in jail right next to Asteio's. And then I'll bust him out. (Oh, and the fact that I smuggled Dev into Asgard and hid him in my room so he can help me. That's the other saving grace.)

This week, with Dev's hacking skills and my demigod connections—okay, fine, mostly Dev's hacking skills—we discovered Ra's evil plan to keep demis locked up in the Black Hole for ridiculous infractions against gods. Slander. (As if the gods don't do that to one another every day.) Throwing away offerings to a deity. (That's just petty, who can tell the difference between a bag of cheese puffs left on the side of the road as an offering for the god of travel and litter? *No one.*) Heresy. (One dude got tossed in the pen for mixing up the names of two Chinese deities: but really for anyone who doesn't speak Chinese, Tianhuang[1] and Tiangong[2] are easy to confuse.)

Ra is an ass.

Dev is currently admiring my shelf full of Animaniacs figurines. He puts his hand out and strokes the back of one of the Goodfeathers pigeons. I leap forward and violate the 'no touching' rule that I have with him.

"Stop!"

"Sorry!" He immediately takes a step back. I quickly grab the figurine and cradle it to my chest.

"This was my sister's," I explain.

"Your sister?"

I hold out my arm and show him the tattoo of the smiling blonde woman there.

"She was a pure human. My half-sister. Dot. She and mom died in a car accident."

I try not to let my emotions take over and drown

me. It happened twenty years ago and I hadn't been in the car, but the trauma of that moment still makes me ache decades later.

I still remember Dad showing up on our farm, trampling through mom's garden, pulling open the back screen door, and slamming me into a fierce hug.

He had sobbed himself into silence before he was able to tell me what was wrong.

I stare down at the little pigeon trio—who are marching along down a shit-stained sidewalk.

"Goodfeathers were Dot's favorite. They gave shit but wouldn't take it. Slappy the Squirrel was a close second for her. She also loved that a character was named after her, of course."

Dev shuffles closer and puts an arm around my shoulders in a gesture of comfort. I stare up at him, the sound of my heartbeat throbbing in my ears.

He's hugging me.

I carefully set down the figurine, so as not to scare him off. Gently, with all the caution that I can muster, I wrap my own hands around his waist. Something in his pants pokes my stomach and I jump back.

"Ow! Dev, you really have got to stop carrying around pencils in your pocket."

Dev clears his throat and turns red, as per usual.

"Sorry. S-s-sorry," he stutters adorably.

I roll my eyes. The boy is too cute for his own good. Just then, Dad's familiar pounding on the door starts. I shoot Dev a look.

"You remember the plan?" I whisper.

He nods.

I fluff my hair and Dev just stands there, staring at me. *Do I have something on my face?* I reach up to check and, then, jerk my head at him, signaling that he needs to hide. Dad might approve of mortal mates for himself, but if he knew what a crush I have on Dev … *his lightning bolts would make daddies with shotguns look like toddlers with kitchen spoons.*

I fling open the door once Dev's hidden under the pile of Animaniac stuffed animals in the corner.

"Greetings, sweetest of all fathers!"

Dad narrows his eyes and peers into the room before looking back at me suspiciously.

"What is it you want? Or, has Loki[3] been in here, scheming with you again?"

I gasp indignantly in mock offense before shooting him my most innocent smile.

"Whatever do you mean?"

His voice is gruff when he commands, "Not tonight, Sigrdrifa."

I sigh, like I'm letting him get his way and he's ruining every ounce of fun that I've planned. "Alright," I offer in pretend supplication.

Unfortunately, Dad knows me better than that— and Uncle Loki and I have been known to pull off some epic stunts in our day.

"Empty your pockets."

My eyes widen and I cross my arms.

"You don't trust me?" I ask rhetorically.

My father snorts.

"You bet your ass that I don't. Your history requires I verify that you're telling the truth."

I roll my eyes but pull out the pockets on my jean shorts. I come up with four pennies and a Kleenex. Dad squints at the pennies in annoyance. It really chafes the gods that human heads are put on coins and not theirs anymore. I've heard drunken dinner rants about how dad's hammer belongs back on a coin at least two dozen times.

"Leave it all behind," he orders.

I toss the pocket detritus onto my nightstand and follow him out, trying not to smirk. Joke's on him—*I've already taped the Visine I plan on using as my biological weapon underneath the dining table at my seat*. I walk amicably down the echoing marble hallway with Dad, cool as a cucumber on the outside, but giddier than a human kid on Christmas.

"How's your week been?" I ask, trying to be friendly.

Dad shakes his head in concern.

"The goats—I worry about them. They were exhausted the other day and I have no idea as to why. I've had to keep a steady stream of servants checking on them. I wish you'd come back to tend them, daughter of mine." He lays a huge hand on my shoulder and pulls me into his side. "They never received better care than when you watched over them."

A trickle of guilt enters my stomach because I know exactly why his goats were worn out—but I quickly squash it because it's not outweighed by the importance of breaking my only childhood friend out of Ra's eternal torture chamber.

All week, I've been asking around about the Black Hole. It seems like *nobody's* ever been released from there. Ra, the bastard Egyptian god, is *setting up* demigods and then raw dogging them in the fart box—*and that's not okay.*

Not in *any* universe.

So, guilt or not, I'm moving forward with my plan.

I sit down at dinner and pretend to eat, but all I really do is wait for the gods to get sufficiently drunk. Aphrodite is sitting next to my father at the end of the table, leaning over so that her breasts nearly spill out of her top as she tells a hilarious story about how the swans that draw her carriage once pecked her husband, Hephaestus, and chased him through the house after he yelled at her for attending an orgy in her honor—*a story I've only heard every single time she's come to our house.*

Poor Hephaestus isn't here to defend himself or add to the story because, well, *how else is Aphwhoredite supposed to seduce my father?*

Once everyone is sufficiently drunk, I reach up and carefully open the boxes of Visine I've taped under the table. I open the flaps and slide out the little bottles. I tuck those into my pockets surreptitiously, using my napkin to hide the lumps. Then, I grab my goblet, because Dad has never adapted to modernities such as *cups*, and head for the drinks table. There's wine there, and also a huge punch bowl filled with a special apple cider.

Idunn[4] makes a batch of this cider from her apples of eternal youth. Without the cider, my family dinners would look like cafeteria hour at a nursing home. Idunn keeps all the gods young and eternally glorious, bless her vanity-soothing heart.

I linger near the wine, using a giant bottle to hide my hands as I unscrew the little vials of Visine. I hope Dev's done his part toward this grand scheme. Technically, mine's enough. But, if you're going to deliberately humiliate a bunch of gods, it's better to take it the full nine yards.

Go big or go home, right?

Loki, the cheeky troublemaker, taught me that.

Once I have the Visine open, I pour some wine into my goblet and move along down the table. I walk slowly, watching the gods. When Aphrodite stands up to tell a story full of gestures and one of her breasts pops out of her draped Grecian gown à la Janet Jackson at the Super Bowl, I know it's my moment.

I quickly empty five vials of Visine into the apple cider. I grab the ladle and give it a quick stir before returning to my seat, where I find Aphrodite has decided not to tuck her boob back in and to sit *on Dad's knee*.

My stepmothers are furious.

Good, I smirk smugly.

Karma's a bitch and my favorite goddess, right now.

It only takes a few minutes before one of my family members shoves away from the table and heads toward the cider. Another soon follows and, over the next half hour, every immortal in the room dips into the cider bowl to imbibe. They immediately look twice as attractive—even my horrid stepsister, Skeggjöld the Skank, and her current shag. I think that he's some god or other from Antartica who was prayed into existence by a ship that got lost there centuries ago.

Enough said, right?

I excuse myself when people around the room start to kiss. It looks like Aphrodite's attempting to turn our family dinner into an orgy ... *classy.*

Oh, and by *classy*, I mean *freaking gross.*

I try not to laugh like a loon as I skip down the hall. This will probably be the most memorable orgy in all of Aphrodite's existence. I doubt she's ever had one interrupted by an immortal case of the runs.

Operation Chocolate Thunder is officially underway when I hear the first, horrific fart rip through the dining room behind me.

It's a true *ass*-plosion.

Sorry, this isn't punny.

Oh, wait, yeah it is!

I clap my hands together in childish glee. I decided, along with Dev, that this was the ironically perfect

crime to get me tossed into the Black Hole, or the Back
Hole, as I've learned that the prisoners call it. I mean, I
am violating the back holes of at least ten gods in that
room back there.

Someone rushes past me for the bathroom. It's my
sister's date. The door on my left slams shut. I stop
walking and wait, listening to a horrid squelching
noise coming from inside the room.

A moment passes before I hear the God of Lost
Shits, I mean *Ships*, boom in an infuriated voice,
"There's no godsdamn toilet paper!"

My face cracks open in mirth.

"Yes! Go Dev!" I whisper as I hurry back to my
room.

Visine was only *part one* of Operation Chocolate
Thunder. But, to really *get their goat*, there's a part two.

Or, *a number two*, if you will.

While I sat through a torturous dinner-slash-orgy-
to-come, Dev was supposed to clear the entire palace
of toilet paper.

Mission accomplished.

6

KHEPRI

Ra's heels click across the prison floor briskly as I follow him to secure the new prisoner. I stare off to one side because if I were to stare directly ahead, I'd be blinded, either by the prima-donna, eighties crimping he has going with his hair, or the sequinned hem of his robe. Ra invented the term flamboyant.

Behind me, I see Raiden right on my tail and I purposefully slow down so that the bastard has to, too. When Ra is present, we walk in rank. Ra, the Tallest and Douchiest—only because his boots have six-inch heels and he's an epic asshole—is first and I follow him. Then, Raiden, who is second-in-rank, followed by whichever guards Ra has tasked to help with this project.

They are nameless, faceless gods who metaphorically suck Ra's cock—apparently, according to Raiden, I eat his ass. As a shit god, I fail to see how this is supposed to offend me. I toss another smirk over my shoulder and quickly stop to brush a non-existent piece of shit off my pant leg before straightening up again. Raiden curses as he stumbles to a stop, trying not to trip over my bent ass.

Yeah, fucker, kiss that.

I quickly start walking again as Ra pivots around just in time to see Raiden push himself up off the floor. The Japanese god looks like he wants to lunge at me. I'm filled with glee.

Try it.

"Raiden-Sama!" Ra snaps. "Can you not march today?"

Raiden glares daggers into my back as he replies, "Apologies, Warden of the Worthless Ones."

Ra sniffs, as if truly offended, and stomps off.

Of course, we follow, but I don't dick around with Raiden anymore. My stomach is churning with concealed rage for what Raiden called Ra—not because I'm upset on Ra's behalf. The self-absorbed bastard is gonna get what's coming to him, mark my words. No, I'm pissed on behalf of the prisoners.

Fuck, if we're being honest, I'm pissed on my behalf, too.

I'm sick of being treated like a piece of shit—ironic, I know—and of everyone being held in this jail being treated like crap simply because they are half-human. As if they could help it.

Raiden's such a micropenis. All his comments about

me taking it from Ra stem from his desire to burn his mouth on the sun god's dick himself.

Ra knows the real score. Fuck, he's the one keeping it. These demigods are powerful—they just don't know it. Ra specifically crafted this jail to drain them of their powers. The sun fucker is afraid of them—and he should be. He's still got a decent percentage of the solar worship because of human obsession with the pyramids and stuff. But if he wasn't siphoning powers, would he really be that strong?

When I finally free the Demigodling, I'm going to annihilate Ra. I think he'd look amazing trapped in a solar storm for the rest of eternity.

Hopefully, Raiden will be indisposed at the time to make my job easier. He's the only god working at the jail that I honestly think would be able to foil my plans. But, I've still got a few more days of working out the kinks before I attempt to spring out Nut's son. As long as no new problems arise …

Ra stops at the elaborate employee entrance to the Back Hole. Prisoners? They see a regular prison, but the employee entrance? You would think you were entering a godsdamn palace, not a prison, when first walking in. Of course, it's decorated in sun symbols and Ra statues—his own little Temple of Doom. For some reason, lots of gods like to give evil a pretty face. They think that makes it better or something.

Waiting there are Anubis' bitches—*seriously*. The jackals are his female lackeys. They have long necks and tall pointed ears that stick straight up. One of them whines when they see Ra. See, I'm not being snide about them being a bunch of females dogs—*just honest.*

And that's where I see my biggest fucking problem yet.

Her.

She stands in the concrete and iron holding cell for new prisoners. She's tall for a woman—almost as tall as Raiden and me, but likely taller than Ra. For some odd reason, this fills me with smug satisfaction. The woman's hair is long, hanging down her back nearly to her waist, and is a glossy chestnut in color. Her skin is fair, indicating she's a northern goddess of some sort, and her eyes are a soft grey-blue mix, like a cloud in the early morning just before the sun kisses it and turns it a pale gold.

When those eyes meet mine, she wrinkles her little button nose and purses her full red lips to give me a scowl that makes my dick harder than advanced calculus. Fuck—this one is definitely going to be trouble. Behind me, I hear Raiden's quick intake of breath and I sniff the air before a smug smile turns my lips upward.

So—*Mr. Roboto likes her, too.*

My beetle senses are acute, even in human form. I can smell a pile of shit ten miles away—don't act like you're not impressed—and everything in between, like pheromones. If Raiden has a hard-on for the new inmate—not that I blame him—it just gives me something else to use against him.

Truly, his attraction amuses me. Raiden-Sama is much too "honorable" (read total dog turd) and too proud to act upon this new desire. Because he'd never stoop to touching someone with mixed heritage.

I nearly laugh out loud. This must be killing the rule-following bastard. What doesn't amuse me is the scent of Ra's attraction on the air—that nearly makes me puke.

In all my time here, I've never smelled Ra's pheromones—thank fuck. He wasn't attracted to any of the guards, let alone the inmates. We are all beneath him and not worthy of his sunny pecker. But, whereas Raiden will bury this shameful temptation, I know Ra will seek out this woman and try to personally destroy her for making him feel something—even lust—for a 'creature' (dickwad sun god's word, not mine) of her status.

Son of a hippo, I think my breakout timeline just ramped up.

Ra is eyeing her with menace. Nothing new, but I understand the deadly intent behind it. The sun prick hasn't made any particular prisoner his personal target except the Demigodling. And, now, her.

I try not to groan at this new headache.

It's going to be a true pain in my ass to keep Ra off of hers the next day or so while I try to rework an escape plan. I hope Thoth has his thinking cap on to help me figure out that final booby trap. For now, I'll have to intervene—strategically.

53

At this point during a normal intake, Ra would have already turned his back on the new inmate, effectively giving him or her his middle finger. Of course, with her, he does no such thing. It's going to take everything that I have to divert his attention.

But, I've got a trick up my sleeve where Ra-fuck is concerned.

He saunters over to the glaring beauty and I realize that I'm silently pleading with her to act submissive— which is definitely a lost cause. There's nothing compliant about the gorgeous vision in front of me and, in truth, I think that's what attracts me most. She has a fire that I doubt even Ra or the Back Hole can put out.

And I hope she fucking incinerates this hell hole if I don't first.

Ra reaches out a hand to trace the curve of her cheek and I see her flinch imperceptibly. I loosen my stance so that Raiden doesn't see my muscles tense—I won't give him anything to use against me, but by the gods, I long to smack Ra's hand away.

"So, you're Thor's troublesome human daughter," Ra drawls menacingly, still touching her. "What was your name again? It was a mouthful. Hmm, perhaps that's what I'll call you—Mouthful."

Ra's leer intensifies, but my new fascination just smirks.

"Yeah, Sigrdrifa is a mouthful. It actually means 'Valkyrie of Dick-Slaying' in Norse, but Mouthful works, too. I do have a mouthful of teeth that can easily replace my penis-chopping ax," she smarts-off with a sassy grin. She follows the grin up by using her tongue to trace over her top teeth.

Fuuuuuuuuck, I'm going to give this woman an earful when we're alone about acting obedient. I refuse to think about wanting to give her a mouthful—that makes me just as bad as Ra (fucking shudder). The sunny douche seems stunned by Thor's daughter's snark and his soft touch suddenly becomes cruel and biting, if her wince is any indication.

"I will teach you some manners, you whor—"

I clear my throat.

"Lord of Iunu[1]," I interrupt with the utmost respect, bowing forward slightly, "do not forget your business with Atum."

Ra's startled gaze flies to mine and he momentarily forgets the new inmate and his would-be wrath at me for intervening.

"What business?" he barks.

I cringe melodramatically.

"Oh, Great King of the Universe, I must have forgotten—and for such, I must be beaten—but Atum is trying to gain back his powers from you. Even as we speak, he is finding other gods to support his cause. It's a despicable plot to overthrow your rule," I moan.

Behind me, Raiden snorts at my theatrics. Even the woman looks at me askance, but Ra eats up my shitty performance like a scarab gobbles up crap. A dark scowl mars his brow as he turns from the new inmate.

"Take this ... insubordinate prisoner away."

Raiden jumps in immediately.

"I can punish her for her insubordination." If possible, his dick tents even harder in his uniform.

Ra's face hardens, his hooked nose scrunching.

"No. I will deal with her when I return."

Ha ha. I know exactly what kind of punishment Raiden wanted to give her, and now he's shit out of luck. Good.

Ra must have seen the hint of desire Raiden tried to hide. I'm not the only one who sucks at acting.

With a snap, Ra vanishes.

Good fucking riddance.

Time for Khepri to be in charge ... but this means I have to be an even bigger asshole to ... whatever her name is.

"What is your name?" I demand gruffly.

"Fuck off," she snaps right back.

"Thor named you Fuck Off? Not very traditional, but it has a nice ring," I comment sarcastically, putting on the asshole song and dance that's expected of me. "Alrighty then, Fuck Off, follow me. Raiden, you follow Fuck Off."

I grin manically at this new offense to the Japanese god until I realize that this will let Raiden stare at her ass the entire march back to her cell. Then, I scowl.

"Actually, Fuck Off, you walk with me. I don't trust you."

I tug her hand until she stumbles next to me. A zing of electricity zips through my flesh at our contact and I nearly groan. *Gods help me to get through the next few days,* I pray to no one in particular.

And, as always, no one answers. When you're a god, prayers don't work. No supernatural figure is gonna swoop in and save my ass.

I'm on my own in this shithole.

No, you're not, my dick reminds me. *Now, you've got her.*

What the hell?

Her?

No.

I just met *her*—I definitely don't have her.

Yet, my dick says.

Fuck me.

My heart speeds up. I quickly let go of her hand and brusquely growl at her to keep up.

I need to get in contact with Thoth immediately. My timeline just moved from a couple of days to now.

Shit gets real when your cock starts talking to you.

7

VAL

I STUMBLE OVER MY OWN TWO FEET TRYING TO KEEP UP with the man I assume is the head guard. His looks are reminiscent of Ra's, the warden, but different. Whereas Ra has the classic Egyptian looks—long black hair, black eyes, dark eyeliner, bronzed shiny skin, etc., etc.—the head guard really only sports the black eyeliner.

His eyes are a startlingly deep blue against the rich contrast of his skin, which is many shades darker than Ra's and the other guard behind me who's dressed in samurai silk. The head guard's hair is black, but it is cropped short to his head. His lips are full, like Ra's, but don't hold the same sadistic sneer that makes my skin crawl.

In fact, for all his bark, I swear that I could see something else dancing in his eyes ...

Interest.

Mischief.

Warning?

I don't freaking know, but it's nothing like what I saw in the Back Hole's turden—*I mean warden*. A lot of things don't scare me, Dad made me run lightning courses as a kid and that knocks a lot of fear out of you, but Ra terrifies me. He has a manic look that screams unhinged, and everyone knows that it's the Kim Jong-Il's that are the most dangerous. That type of deranged unpredictability mixed with an absolute lack of empathy equals death. Lots of death.

Or getting a mouthful while you're on your knees in some dingy corner of The Rectum.

No, thank you.

I've got to think of a way to make myself less attractive to Ra.

The head guard—I'm going to call him Bi-Polar for that whole hand-holding, dropping thing—takes a sharp right without warning. My brain doesn't compute the move initially and my legs keep marching forward until I feel a slight tug on the back of my shirt —another Animaniacs tee, this time with Dot on it. It was my sister's so it's washed and faded to the point that it's practically white. And I had to cut a whole out of the bottom so it's been converted into a crop top. But still, it's hers and I always feel like I can do anything when I wear it.

I look behind me to see the ninja guard pulling me in the direction that Bi-Polar went.

"This way," he commands curtly.

His eyes rove over my face almost ... hungrily, but he seems the most put out by my presence. Possibly even more pissed than Raw-Eggs for brains who runs the place. When I don't move, he places a hand on my elbow and the same crazy tingle that I felt with Bi-Polar starts humming underneath my skin at Kung Fu's —as I'm dubbing him—touch. My eyes fly to his in shock, and he drops the façade for a moment. I catch a fleeting glimpse of the man on the inside that probably never sees the light of day if the stern scowl perpetually etched on his face is any indication.

For some inexplicable reason, I'm drawn to this enigma wrapped up in a god.

"Do you ever sumo wrestle?" I suddenly blurt out, my mind briefly envisioning him in the scantily clad uniform of the fighters. He's definitely not built like a stereotypical sumo wrestler. He's thin and I can see the bulge of biceps underneath his sleeves.

I can't be sure, but I think that my little fantasy has properly done justice to his tightly bronzed ass cheeks. Of course, I can't be sure unless I see them in real life ...

Earth to Val!

What the hell is wrong with me?!

Does the Egyptian underworld fuck with your mind so much that you lose it within seconds of being here?

I don't check out gods—*and I sure as hell don't check out gods who work at The Shit Pincher.*

Behind me, Bi-Polar has come sauntering back. He's

slick as oil, but there's something menacing in his expression when I glance up and find his eyes locked on the spot where Kung Fu is still touching me. But, he plays it off well, laughing even.

"Did she just call you fat, Raiden-Sama?" he taunts.

"Fuck off, Khepri!" Kung Fu—apparently Raiden-Sama, although I like my name better—snaps.

"Are you telling me to 'fuck off' or are you talking to her?" Khepri, a.k.a. Bi-Polar, continues.

Bi-Polar doesn't wait for an answer, but wrenches me from Kung Fu's grasp instead. Kung Fu grabs me right back. They engage in a mini tug-of-war with me as the rope. I should be annoyed but all I can think about is both of their hands touching me at once and my body immediately goes into overdrive.

"Let go!"

"I've got her, you let go!" Bi-Polar growls. Damn, that growl sends warm sunshine straight down my spine to my—

"I had her first."

"You don't get anything first. You get it when I say you get it. And you don't get to touch her," Bi-Polar yanks me again so that my cheek smashes into his hard pecs. His nipple digs into my forehead like a rock.

I wonder if he's the kind of god who's into nipple play.

Kung Fu pulls me back and digs his other hand into my hips. I can feel something hard press into my back. Is that his knife in its sheath or …

The hallway fills with testosterone. And gods' testosterone is intense. It's a feral thing, especially when the gods are feeling possessive. It creates a wild cloud that can lead to war, murder, or orgies on a prison floor.

The prisoners around us start to hit tin cans against the bars. Some chant, "Fight her!"

Others scream, "Fuck her!"

The two gods move closer, going nose to nose as they argue with one another. I end up smashed between them, one hand pressed against Bi-Polar's abs and the other twisted behind my back, smashed between me and the chiseled planes of Kung Fu's chest.

The two shout at one another, but I can't hear anything. I'm drenched in testosterone, reeling from it. My body feels like it's on fire and, then, out of nowhere, the orgasm of the century crashes over me. Heat slides from my lower regions up my spine and makes my eyes roll. My knees buckle at the force of it and it takes everything inside of me not to cry out like a whore working for her money.

Holy hades. Did that just happen? Valhalla take me.
It did.

As if that weren't humiliating enough, both men immediately release me and I do collapse to the ground —a puddle of endorphins at their feet. Kung Fu clears his throat, but Bi-Polar stares at me with hooded eyes, his nostrils flaring widely like … Like he can smell what just happened.

Oh, gods.

Just stay quiet, Val, just stay quiet.

I chant this over and over to myself, but do I listen?

Do I ever freaking listen?!

"Can you smell orgasms?!" I burst out incredulously.

Oh shit.

Dev would totally punch me right now if he heard me say that.

I want to punch me for saying it out loud.

What happened to my internal filter—*did the orgasm shatter it?*

Kung Fu lets out a low, deep moan and Bi-Polar's eye starts to twitch.

"We need to get her to her cell now," he tells Kung Fu instead of answering me—*which might be for the best.*

Both men grasp a small portion of my sleeve and practically run down the hallway as I trip along in their grasp.

Prisoners hoot and holler behind us, whistles echoing off the dim prison walls.

The two guards are very careful not to touch me again. I'm not sure if I'm relieved or not. An image of Dev flashes through my brain and I'm instantly swamped with guilt.

Dev—*my dream boyfriend, the one that I left back in Asgard.*

We reach my cell before guilt renders me immobile, and Dick One and Dick Two, as I'm now calling them (partially because I'm furious at them and partially because I can't stop imagining what their dicks look like), unceremoniously shove me inside. They each stomp off in opposite directions, but without a backward glance at me, so I pop both my middle fingers up at their departing backs.

Fucking gods! They're probably arrogant human-haters. But then part of me wonders if they are fucking gods ... to make me have that kind of an orgasm, they must have some kind of lust power, right?

I'm so frazzled that I barely take stock of the other inmate in my new home.

My thoughts are stuck on Dev and my arrest.

It happened so quickly—quicker than I expected. I barely had time to reconvene with Dev and snag Mjölnir. That's right ...

I stole my father's infamous hammer.

How the hell else am I supposed to break out of The Sphincter?

Certainly not by using my non-existent god powers.

I need that hammer to ram the Back Hole so hard that it flops open bigger than a sausage alley and lets all of us demis stream out.

I feel terrible for taking it—I feel even worse for making my father sick from the Visine. I love him; the others I could give a fuck less about and, as gods, everyone recovered four times as fast as a human would have. Which explains why I'd hardly had time to shrink Mjölnir and shove it into my bra before Ra's minions were there to haul me away.

My amusement at seeing my stepmoms pale, shaking, and a little gassy was replaced with guilt at the profound look of sadness on Dad's face.

And the fact that I didn't even get to tell Dev goodbye.

But, Dev is one in a million—even in the god world. He'll find a way out of Asgard just like I'll find a way out of The Butt Hole with Asteio. All I need to do is get the lay of the land and some allies. I turn to my cellmate now, finally taking him in.

What the heck are they feeding everyone here?!

He's tall and muscular, with tanned skin and a six pack that looks as hard as stone. His inky hair is cropped on the top, but long on the sides and the back ...

A mullet has never looked so sexy, I freaking swear.

And when he turns his eyes on me?

Holy shit.

It must be something in the undead water of Duat because my body flares to life just like it did for Kung Fu and Bi-Polar.

Let's just hope that this demigod can't smell orgasms, too.

8

THE ORIGINAL TUPAC

Two Minutes and Four Seconds Earlier …

That Raiden dickwad moved Squirrel Tail out of my cell a couple of hours ago. I don't think he liked us getting drunk on the regular. We did get a bit loud when we imbibed.

I lay back on my bunk and regret that Squirrelly was moved washes over me. I am gonna miss him.

Luckily for me, he did give me a parting gift. A toilet bowl full of wine. Don't judge. If you'd been in prison for four hundred years, seventy five days, twelve hours, and six minutes, you'd happily drink from a toilet, too.

How did I do that fast math?

I'm a Sun demigod.

Even if I can't see the sun, I can feel it. I know every second that passes—which is possibly worse than not knowing.

Ra was quick to take out any other part-solar deities. And since Daddio's the Incan Sun God, whelp, my head was on the chopping block before you could say Inti.[1]

I sigh and lean back against my bed, wondering who they'll bring in next. Hopefully, it's not the demigod of flatulence again. He was an *awful* roommate—and not just because of the smell. He had a rotten attitude that went right along with his scent.

Squirrel Tail and I must have pushed it too much the other night when we dared the inmates in the cell across the hall to a dick-dancing contest. I won, of course. I've been in a cell for longer than most of these other demis, so I've had all the time in the world to practice twerking my rod. As a result, my dick can karate chop better than Jackie Chan. Yeah, I know who that is. Sometimes that Khepri dude "loses" his phone and we can stream shows. He's not a totally evil guy—for a god.

Or a guard.

Watching shows on his phone is one of the only perks in this place.

That and I-Scream night.

It's not what you're thinking—the cold, delicious human treat that I've seen made and eaten on TV. I-

Scream night is the night that Ra picks an unlucky demi to torture. We all take bets on how long it's gonna take the poor bastard to scream.

Heartless?

Abso-fucking-lutely.

But after centuries in the dark with little to do other than rip your sheets into tiny strips and attempt to make homemade macrame,[2] you kind of lose a little bit of your own sense of humanity.

I miss the sun.

Not just my father, the sun god, but the actual warmth and light of the sun.

When Squirrel Tail came, it was almost like I got a little piece of my humanity back. He was brand new to the jail, full of stories and life. And a shit ton of ass hair. That's how he got his nickname. It was so bushy, even when he was in full human form and not trotting around as a half-goat man, his ass-hair curled out of his crack like a tail. That bushy tail even beat out the fact that my roomie could shoot wine from his fingertips, if it gives you any idea just how impressive the fur was.

Asteio was his real name, but nobody calls anyone by real names here. That just leads to a lot of nostalgia, which is bad when you never get visitors and have a sentence lasting all eternity.

In fact, that very thought kind of brings me down. And normally, I've got a pretty sunny disposition—pun totally intended.

Across the hall, Blimpy, a chubby demigod, son of Nomkhubulwane[3] calls out, "Sunny, dick dancing rematch. Tonight!"

I sit up and wave a hand at him.

"Sure. Sure."

But further conversation cuts off when I hear footsteps. I stand up in my cell. It's never a good idea to meet a new demi lying down—some fight for dominance or other bullshit like that.

My jaw drops when I see my new cellmate.

Holy shit!

They're giving me a woman?!

And not any woman—a scorching one with thick brunette hair and breasts as delicious and ripe as passion fruit, jiggling slightly under her prison-issued orange sweatshirt. I gulp when my eyes travel down and I realize they haven't bothered to make her change out of her street clothes. She is wearing the tiniest shorts known to man.

Thank the gods—every single one.

I want to—*no*, I *need* to run my tongue up and down over those smooth, creamy legs.

Right.

Fucking.

Now.

I run my tongue over my teeth, glad I brushed this morning. I quickly check my embroidered loincloth—I don't do prison uniforms. I'm damn glad that I'm sporting my yellow pair today. There's a sun embroidered over the crotch and a red chevron pattern over each leg. It's one of my favorites. I brush my mullet aside, determined to make a good impression.

I take a step back as the guards push her inside.

She stumbles a little, her rough work boots scuffing against the stone floor. She turns and glares out at them, not acknowledging me for a second, but giving me time to admire the curve of her ass.

Oh, sweet demi-goddess.

This woman has got to be the daughter of some lust god because, right now, the sun on my loincloth has risen. My dick is hard in a way it hasn't been *in centuries.*

That ass is worth a thousand poems; it would make her a principal wife any day.[4]

But she seems upset, and I don't want to 'fuck up' any chance I might have with her. So, I make my sunset the best I can by focusing on a bug crawling across the wall—nothing like staring at a beetle to make your cock shrivel.

I clear my throat and my new soulmate—cellmate— turns to look at me.

Her eyes are a gorgeous blue and strike at me like lightning, sending electric thrills through my veins and raising all the hair on my arms.

Mr. Sun starts to come to attention again.

No!

Down boy!

I slide one hand down to shield my Magic Mike from view as I put the other forward to shake.

"Hey, I'm Tupac."

"Like the singer?" the demigoddess asks as she takes my hand.

Her skin feels softer than butter against mine, but she's hit on a sore point.

"Nothing like him. He's an imposter. Or *was*."

I can't help but curl my lip—that stupid rapper has transformed *all* my glory into dark rhyming slurs. No one can hear my name anymore without thinking of feuds and mayhem when all I am about is calm and nature. I was a farmer before I was taken but, apparently, being a gangster is more glamorous.

More worthy of google searches.

I have to resist blowing a raspberry.

"His music was C-R-A-P." *(See what I did there? I'm pretty proud of myself.)* "I was around for centuries before he was."

My cellie's eyebrows shoot up.

"Oh, so, you're ancient. Wow. I'm only twenty-seven."

Her eyes flicker around the cell and she sits down on my bed.

The sight of her on my bed sets off a whole new round of *sunrise, sunset*.

Fuck me.

(I wish she would.)

"I'm Val."

"Val."

I let her name roll around in my mouth like chocolate—*it sounds just as decadent.*

"So, um, Tupac, sir … I mean … um, how do you prefer to be addressed? Your Radiance? Mr. Tupac? *Grandpa?*"

She bites her lip.

I swallow hard. She didn't just *sir* me. *Why is she being all respectful?* Horror rushes through me—does she think I'm *old*?! My libido falls to his knees like Marlon Brando crying 'Stella!'—this cannot be happening! We're demis. We live thousands of years; some of us are even immortal. Surely she's slept with someone fifty times her age before—oh, just that thought makes my sun throb in angry heat. Nope.

Can't picture that—*don't want to.*

But if she is *that* innocent … my mind whirls at all the delicious ways I could corrupt her. I can show her that centuries of experience are a good thing—*not a bad thing.* I wonder if she's read the human book *Twilight*—that got passed around the prison like an STD (As did *Fifty Shades of Gray*—I liked *Twilight* better). I try to remember who has the copy now as I answer her.

"You can just call me Tupac, though my prison nickname is *Lover*," I purr seductively with a smile as bright as midday.

"No, it's not!" Blimpy yells from his cell.

I turn to see him standing at the bars, staring at Val

like she's the first rain cloud to travel through the desert sky in months.

I step in the way of his view.

"Don't listen to Blimpy," I tell her. "So, what trumped up charge are you in for?"

Val grins.

"Oh, it's not trumped up. I gave all the gods of Asgard the runs and hid the toilet paper—it was a literal shit storm," she laughs.

I cock my head, confused.

"But …"

Her smile widens.

"I got arrested *on purpose*," she clarifies.

"Why would you want to come here?!"

I'm eternally grateful she's here—*but that makes zero sense*.

"Because …" Val's explanation, whatever it is, gets lost when she reaches down the middle of her shirt and touches her boobs.

Ohhhhhhhhhhhh.

Fuck yes.

But she doesn't start to tweak her nipples like I'm hoping.

Instead, she pulls something out of her shirt—and it's not her bra.

Huge sigh of disappointment.

It's a hammer … a tiny, two inch tall hammer—like a child's toy.

I blink and try to clear my head from the gutter, I mean its confusion.

"I'm sorry, what did you just say?"

Val's grin grows wider.

"I said—*I'm gonna bust us all out of here.*"

It dawns on me she doesn't mean *bust a nut*—this *Chiquita Banana has an escape plan.*

9

VAL

I WATCH DAD'S HAMMER GROW IN MY HANDS UNTIL IT'S A giant mallet, still marveling at the fact that Mjölnir let me pick it up in the first place. That was, by far, the trickiest part of my plan because Mjoli seems to have a conscious mind of its own—only the worthy can pick it up and all that.

I'd wrapped my hand in one of Dad's old t-shirts just in case, but Mjoli had come along nice and easy and when I'd whispered to ask it to shrink, it had. The huge-ass sentient hammer had shrunk to the size of a toothpick and let me shove it in my bra. Once there, I'd heard a little creak and the metal had gently wrapped around my breast like an underwire. Part of me had wondered if Mjoli's conscience was male at that point but, ultimately, it didn't matter. What mattered was that I break Asteio out of Ra's turd of a prison.

I use Mjoli to smash the cuffs chained around my

ankles; then, I stand in my cell. My tall, swoon-worthy, and incredibly old cellmate gapes at me as I study the welds on the hinges.

"What is that?" he breathes.

I don't answer. I change the subject. If this fails, I might still be able to hide my weapon and try again. But I definitely won't be able to do anything if he spills the beans. "Do you know how to get outside?" I ask him. "If I break down the cell door, do you know the way?"

Lover just shakes his head. I can't call him Tupac in my head—that just gets too confusing because Dot had liked rap music. So, Lover it is—even though that feels like a weird thing to say to a guy who walks around in patterned underwear. I don't think he's gotten the memo that only seven-year-old girls wear suns on their panties. But that's what happens when you are a demigod who's old—you lose touch with reality ... and what's hip.

I swallow the thought that I will one day be that embarrassing. Then, I decide I'm being just as petty as my step sister, Skanky. And that is a definite no-go in my book. Number one life goal: Do *not* be Skanky. So, I shove aside any judgement against Lover, who has been nothing but welcoming since I arrived. He didn't even challenge me to a prison fight or anything, even though I could tell I sat down on his bed. It smelled like him, like warmth and fresh streams somehow, which should be impossible in this dark place—but demigods can often do impossible things.

I turn back to the hinges on our cell door to study them some more. They look normal enough, but with gods, you can never tell. Ra isn't known as a trickster god, thank goodness. If Uncle Loki had built a prison, it would be much harder to break out of—I can guarantee that.

As I bend forward to inspect the bottom hinge, Lover squeaks behind me.

Did he stub his toe?

I don't turn to look because some heavy set dude from across the hall sticks an arm through his cell. "Psst. Hey gorgeous, if you free yourselves, would you mind freeing me too?"

I look over at him and then back at the hinges. "That's the plan. Full scale prison riot."

I lift the hammer, about to take a swing, when this beetle on the wall flies into my face. And—like most girls—I frickin' shriek and step back.

I squawk again when the beetle starts to transform into a man. I watch as wings turn into arms and its spindly insect legs grow into tall, muscled pillars.

Shit!

I thought this prison stifled most demigod magic! At least … it stifled the magic that would help them escape.

Becoming a beetle would definitely make that list.

Which means this isn't a demigod.

It's a god. Only full god magic isn't stifled in this prison. It's why I brought the hammer.

Lover and I are both frozen in place as magic swirls around us and a devastatingly handsome god presses against my chest.

Not just any god, the hot Egyptian prison guard who'd just made me orgasm like my afterlife (not just my life, but my *freaking eternity*) depended on it.

My cheeks flame.

Dammit.

It's Bi-Polar.

I'm caught before I even got started.

Lover gives a screech and charges at the guard, shouting, "Run, Val!"

That definitely earns him chivalry points.

Lover slams into the Bi-Polar and pins him to the wall for a second, before the guard turns his deep blue, kohl-lined eyes to me. "I will help you."

My eyes widen.

Lover chuckles and slams the guard harder into the stone wall. I can't help how my eyes slip to see how well-defined Lover's ass is. There's no embroidery blocking the rear view and his muscled ass cheeks flex as he holds the full god against the wall.

"Yeah, right. Why would you help us escape? I've been here for centuries, Khepri," Lover snarls.

I look back at the full god, whose eyes flare with heat.

"I've been planning a break out for centuries."

"Right," Lover drawls sarcastically.

"You don't know the maze he's created. I do. Ra isn't here right now. And we'd best leave before he returns. But we need to take at least one other prisoner with us. The Demigodling. I promised his mother I'd free him."

Lover drops Bi-Polar but takes up a fighting stance.

"Bullshit. Why should we believe any of this?"

I grip Mjoli tighter. "I'm with the ancient dude on this one. Why now?"

Bi-Polar's mouth settles into a thin line.

"I'm far more ancient than Tupac and, as such, I know Ra well. I could feel his wrath underneath the interest he showed in you. When he gets back, he will call for you. And you will wish you were never born. I don't want that for you."

His voice takes on an urgent tone.

Did my orgasm mean that much to him?

Or is there something about the prison magic that draws everyone together?

Does the drain that Ra put on demigod magic have some unknown, horny side effect?

Lover's arm goes around me protectively. His bicep feels strong across my back and his hand brushes the side of my jean shorts in a familiar way, like we're friends (or more), even though we just met moments ago. This reinforces my theory.

"Let Ra take me instead when he gets back," my cellmate offers.

That second bit of chivalry hits me right in the lady

bits. I mean, a guy willing to take on torture for you *should* be a turn on, right?

But it's completely unnecessary. And possibly a little insulting. Does he not believe I can break us out of here?

"We'll be gone before then," I say.

My eyes land on Khepri and narrow.

"If you are really gonna help, you're gonna do everything I say."

"I give you my oath," he promises.

Lover sucks in a breath and I glance over at him.

"Should I believe him?"

Lover nods and tightens his hold, hand squeezing my hip. "An oath by a god is unbreakable. Now ask him for the keys."

"If I unlock all the doors, then Ra will know it was me," Bi-Polar counters. "If she breaks you out, it will at least take him a little longer to try to unravel who did it. We'll have more time to get away"

"Okay then, step back." I say.

"Why don't you let me swing that?" Khepri asks.

I have to bite back a grin.

"Sure thing."

I set Mjoli down and step back, biting down on my smile. This is gonna be fun.

The Egyptian god gives an arrogant smirk before stooping to pick up the hammer one-handed. He can't.

Two handed.

He still can't.

Two hands and a foot propped up on the bars for leverage.

The chubby guy in the cell across the way starts laughing. Lover chuckles. Bi-Polar gets … *bi-polar.*

His eyes flash with fury and he curses Mjoli.

"What the fuck, stupid hammer!"

The hammer just doubles in size. Probably Mjoli's idea of a 'fuck you.'

I take pity on Bi-Polar and step forward. "Probably not a good idea to curse him." I've decided Mjoli is definitely a guy.

So I grab his shaft gently and caress it up and down a second. "Hey, sweet thing, you ready to bust us out?" I whisper to the hammer. I'm not certain, but it feels like the handle grows a little thicker under my touch. But I'm easily able to lift it, and then it almost swings itself, smashing into the top hinge with full force. One more swing and my cell door falls down in front of me.

The guys immediately rush forward, but I hold up a hand to stop them. "Wait inside, please." I lift the hammer to my lips, give it a little kiss, and step into the hall and throw it.

Mjoli spins as fast as a throwing star, hitting the lock on every cell door on the right before twisting like a boomerang and coming back on the left side, smashing through every lock there before returning to my hand. Two more throws and all the hinges are gone too so that the guards can't just toss people back inside and easily lock them up.

Cell doors fall like dominos.

Demigods rush out into the hall and turn to look at me.

I smile once Mjoli's back in my hand. "Hey peeps. Time for a premature evacuation!"

10

RAIDEN

I'M RUNNING A QUICK PERIMETER CHECK OUTSIDE THE jail, ruminating about *her* and what happened. I'm still confused about what entirely transpired. All I know— the Nordic seductress is in my head and I can't get her out of it. That alone makes me equal parts furious and sick to my stomach. In fact, the more I think about it, the more I'm convinced that some enemy of my family has cursed me.

It's the only thing that makes sense—*why else would I be sexually attracted to an ill-begotten deviant?!*

I try to ignore how innocent she looked and focus on the fact that she's a half-breed and was placed in The Black Hole for good reason. Ra doesn't imprison innocent demis. Each one of them has perpetrated some heinous crime against the gods—*an unspeakable travesty in itself*. I can only assume that their human side makes them less reasonable and more reckless.

Makes me wonder if Khepri the Brainless isn't a demi.

I kick the barbed wire topped wall in annoyance at the thought of him, our confrontation, and *her* reaction.

Khepri, the little fuck, finally decides to quit acting like a pussy and fight back like a man and, when I engage him, she steps between us and *fucking comes* when we both make contact with her. This troublemaking little demi, whose pheromones were already permeating my brain, had *an orgasm* when Kheprick *and I* touched her—an orgasm that smelled better than a rainstorm.

My brain keeps repeating this over and over, like it can't quite understand. My dick understands well enough, though, and is more than happy to toss aside our honor, familial duty, and morals for a go at the girl. *Damn whoever cursed me! They can go straight to Yomi!*[1]

I kick the wall again and allow my anger to leak out into the atmosphere. I hear thunder in the distance—a reaction to my unchecked emotions, but I hear something else, too. Something that I can't quite put my finger on.

I take a calming breath and the thunder subsides, but the other noise only grows louder. It's a strange clanking sound.

I realize that it's coming from *inside the prison*. I stare at the very modern human-looking jail—Ra specifically made it this way to remind the prisoners of their dirty human heritage.

I hear the noise again. A repeated clank. Almost rhythmic.

I rush inside, instinctively going to the new inmate's cell. I'm one hundred percent certain that whatever is happening is due to the new troublemaker. I descend two flights of stairs and make my way through three secret passages to get to her floor as quickly as possible. When I round a corner, chaos greets me and I'm shoved aside by the sea of escaping inmates running amok.

That's right—*fucking inmates running amok.*

My anger comes roaring back to life and I unheedingly unleash it on the criminals. Thunder crashes overhead and lightning arcs from inmate to inmate, incapacitating them. They fall to the ground, limbs wiggling like the Jello-jigglers that Zaca[2] brought to my parents last dinner party as a joke. I will electrocute every one of these fucks and then drown them for shits and giggles.

Since they are demis, they can't be killed, but I can get some enjoyment from their mass mutiny. My thoughts scatter when, suddenly, *she* comes walking toward me. Like Moses, another demifuck, she parts the throngs of inmates in two and walks tranquilly down the path she's made for herself. I absently note that my lightning is not affecting her at all, but then, I remember that she's Thor's daughter.

Of course, she's immune to my kind of electricity.

I should try something else to disarm her ... my dick offers to toss her some of his skills.

I doubt throwing her some meat will weaken her, you asshole, I sneer at my traitorous cock.

Doesn't hurt to try, comes his ballsy response.

My brain agrees. It wouldn't hurt to try—*it wouldn't hurt at all* ... in fact, trying would do the opposite of hurt, a phantom orgasm floats up and clouds my thoughts.

The object of my obsession comes to a halt when she finally reaches me. I'm only a smidge taller than her and I try not to focus on her long, gorgeous legs. Instead, I stare intently upon her face and pray that she keeps her outspoken mouth shut.

Gods only know if she talks about smelling her orgasm how long I'll be able to hold out before I break down and beg to lick her pussy or something equally disturbing—even in the midst of a breakout, I can't stay focused on anything more than her.

I'm going to seriously fuck up whoever had the guts to dishonor my family and me with this attraction jinx, but my thoughts trail off when the Nordic demi stops in front of me. She tips back her head and smiles sweetly up at me.

Innocently.

Maybe Ra *did* make a mistake.

Then, she raises a tiny little hammer. It can't be bigger than her index finger. It looks kind of cute in her hand—*until she smashes it into the side of my left temple.* I roar in pain as my vision instantly starts to tunnel. My last thought before everything goes black:

Not innocent.

But still fuckable, my dick throws in.

Of course, *it* gets the last word before I go unconscious.

WHEN I COME TO, EVERYTHING IS HAZY AND I'M confused as to where I am … hell, I can barely remember *who* I am. All around me, people are sprinting and rejoicing, the boisterous sounds bounce off the rock walls and I squint. Maybe I'm at a party? Three people surround me—two guys and a lovely woman. For some reason, they are all familiar to me, especially the one man wearing eyeliner, but I can't seem to be able to place them.

"Hi," I yell, startling the brunette woman into dropping what looks like a small hammer pick. "Can you tell me who you are, where I'm at, and who I am?"

"What?" the woman squeaks, but the familiar man just laughs maniacally.

"You concussed him, Fuck-Off, congrats!" he tells the woman named Fuck-Off.

"What's concussed?" I wonder.

I watch a man next to me leap down the hall shouting, "I'm free! I'm free!" I'm not exactly sure what he's free from … pain, death, an unhappy marriage? But we're in a long, dark hallway with a lot of broken doors. That doesn't seem right. My head twinges.

"Concussed is nothing you need to worry about now," the other guy, the one with bright yellow underwear, inserts smoothly. "I'm Lover and you're Raiden."

I hold out a hand for him to shake.

"My lover?" I ask, uncertainly.

I'm unsure if I'm into men ... I don't think I am. My gaze keeps wandering to Val, not the others. Next to me, the guy with the kohl-lined blue eyes barks out a laugh at my comment, and Lover smacks me on the back.

"Nah, it's just my nickname, I'm Tupac, but I prefer you to yell 'Lover' if you need me." Lover gives me a grin and a wink.

Behind him, a chubby man shouts, "You gave yourself that nickname!"

Lover turns and shows that man a single middle finger.

"You want us to leave you behind, Blimpy? Then shut the afterlife up!"

I nod toward Lover.

"Nice to meet you. *Raiden*—I like my name." I roll the unfamiliar name around my tongue a few times, trying to get used to it. My eyes flicker around the little circle the others have formed near me.

"So, you're Lover, you're Fuck-Off, and I feel like I know you ..." I tell the familiar-looking handsome man in the white tunic.

He seems to be choking on laughter at something and the woman is frowning fiercely at me.

"*Val.* Please call me Val," she requests, her smile polite even though her eyes are tight.

"Of course," I tell her gallantly. It's only honorable to do as a lady requests. And for some reason, that feels important to me. "I wouldn't want to be called Fuck-Off, either."

"I'm Khepri," the Egyptian guy finally introduces himself.

"Khepri," I say, testing the name. "Huh, never heard it. Do I know you?"

Val gets a secretive smile that I love to watch spread over her expressive face. That little grin causes my heart to gather and swell, like clouds before a storm. She's so pretty.

"He's your best friend!" she announces and my bestie looks shocked at her words.

"I'm *so sorry* that I don't remember you," I apologize. I feel embarrassed. What happened that I don't even recall my best friend?! It seems so ... *dishonorable.*

Khepri runs a hand over his face and shoots Val a look before he replies, "It's, ah, no problem. I'm sure your memory will come back with time. Until then, old *friend*, we're breaking out of the hellhole of a jail. Any help you can lend us would be great."

"Yeah!" some woman behind us shouts. "Hurry the hell up before Ra or someone else comes back down here!"

Khepri waves an arm and shouts, "Form a single file line! We're marching up the stairs!"

A line forms behind us and Khepri leads us through a door into another dark, dank hallway where algae has started to grow on one wall from a continuous leak.

"Of course, I'll help! I'm not sure how, but anything for my best friend! Erm—why are we in jail?"

My eyes fly up the dank walls, and I realize that there are no windows in this place. It's so dreary and depressing.

"A bad guy put us here against our will and forced us to eat lima beans," Tupac announces and I shudder.

"Lima beans?" I ask in distaste.

Why can't I remember people but my palate can remember the slimy, disgusting texture of a bean that tastes like rotten dirt?

"Lima beans," Lover confirms.

"Thank the gods we're escaping," I conclude, following them. "This isn't simply a prison, but a torture chamber if they force one to choke down lima beans. Where are we going now?"

"There are still two more people we have to save," Khepri says, "but we're going to have to tread carefully because Ra has set boobytraps throughout the prison that go off when anyone tries to escape."

"Will the others be ok?" Val worries.

Khepri gives an unsure shrug.

"I hope so; there are enough Egyptian demis among the prisoners to help accurately navigate everyone's way out. And, luckily, I can read hieroglyphics, but Ra hasn't made this easy. It's one of the reasons that I've hesitated to release the Demigodling. I wanted to make sure I knew all of Ra's booby traps before attempting his escape."

"You can read the pretty pictures painted on the walls? That's awesome!" I tell him, truly happy to be the best friend of someone so magnificent—I tell him this, too.

Lover seems to find my confession hilarious, though.

"This way," Khepri directs, leading us around a corner. The stairs disappear and the geometric walls become nothing more than a round dirt tunnel that twists in coils through the dirt, lit by an occasional tiny floating ball of fire. We've gone into what seems like the bowels of the jail.

I point this out and Val hoots with laughter.

"The bowels of the Back Hole, ahahahaha!"

"The Back Hole?" I wonder, wrinkling my forehead as I glance over at her.

"That's the name of the prison," Lover supplies.

"Ah," I gasp in understanding, "That is funny!" I laugh with them, stomach shaking—*it feels so good*. For some reason, I get the impression that I haven't laughed in forever.

"STOP!" Khepri suddenly orders and we all stumble to a grinding halt. "The first boobytrap," he intones mysteriously, walking over to a wall that blocks our path forward. It has symbols etched into the side. There are animals, people, eyes, hands, and other shapes I can't identify.

His hand traces the figures from top to bottom. He's silent while he reads and, then, he nods. He turns back to us and says, in a voice that carries down the tunnel to the line of prisoners, "One of these stones will open to reveal the right path—the wrong one is filled with venomous snakes that can incapacitate even gods. According to these hieroglyphics, I need to press this stone."

Khepri the Bestest Friend in the World pushes it and a panel swooshes open, revealing a long, unlit hall that fades into darkness. I clap in praise and Khepri gives me a small bow. Wow—this guy. I secretly want to be just like him.

My clap is echoed down the line behind us until the tunnel is full of applause that sounds like the pitter patter of rain, a most glorious sound.

"Hurry—we need to move before Ra returns," Val directs. "This is the way to Asteio?" she verifies with Khepri, who nods. "Any additional guards?" She reaches into her shirt, pulling the collar down to reveal a delicious amount of cleavage before she pulls out a tiny curved hammer that looks vaguely familiar.

I shake off that familiarity and peer into the dark hallway. I need to focus on helping my best friend, not on trying to remember where I've seen tiny hammers that don't look like they could squash a cherry tomato.

"Here, let me light the way," Lover adds, fire filling his hands and setting the tunnel aglow. He turns back and says to those in line behind us, "Any light or solar demis, spread yourself out so you can provide light for the others!"

Shuffling occurs as the prisoners behind us rearrange themselves.

We walk down in pairs, Khepri and Lover first and then Val and me. I debate taking her elbow, to help her along some of the rockier terrain, but for some reason, the thought of touching her makes my stomach get nervous and jittery.

Suddenly, the two men in front of us abruptly stop.

"Dude—are you sure you can read hieroglyphics?!" Lover accuses.

I hear a loud angry hiss.

"I can read hieroglyphs—Ra just fucked us, is all. Nothing new there. Both paths probably have snakes," Khepri adds bitterly, and I hate this Ra being with all my heart to have tricked my best friend so.

I move in front of Val (it's only honorable to protect the lady) and peer around Lover and see a whole bunch of black serpents slithering out of a hole in the wall to flood the floor. The instant that they hit the ground, they rear back in ire, their mouths open, fangs gleaming, ready to strike at anyone nearby. I remember Khepri's words about how their venom can fell even a god and I frown. I can't let these legless freaks hurt my friends.

"Step aside!" I command gallantly, startling everyone into doing my bidding.

Raising my hands imperiously, I let lightning dance forth from my fingertips until I've fried every last snake. The smell of smoked meat fills my nostrils and I realize that I'm a little hungry. I march over and pick up one singed delicacy before stuffing it in my mouth and munching it down—*bones and all.*

"Did ... did he just *eat* one of those things?!" Val whispers behind me.

"I think it's the least strange thing he's done, considering," Khepri murmurs back.

Am I the strange friend, then? I would have thought Lover was. Khepri's clearly the handsome one.

"I'm hungry from eating just lima beans," I defend and Lover nods understandingly, which I appreciate —*he seems to live up to his name.*

"Hurry up. I want to swallow some snake too," someone yells from the line behind us. "And I'm not talking about the literal kind."

Chuckles and affirmations travel up and down the line at that.

"Let's keep going. I'm sure this is actually the right path," Khepri urges us on.

We walk before coming to a set of descending stairs where Khepri motions for us to pause.

"Another boobytrap," Khepri sighs.

I shake my head in disgust. "This Ra guy is a real cocksucker," I whisper my observation to Val, who nods in agreement with a big grin. For some reason, her grin makes my nerves dance like lighting during a storm.

"Right, basically anyone who walks through here gets speared to death," Khepri declares, reading the new set of glyphs.

"What if a beetle were to fly through?" Val suggests.

I look around in confusion. *Where are we going to get a beetle?*

I turn around just in time to see Khepri shifting into one! I feel my jaw open in shocked admiration. Is there anything this man *can't* do?

He flits down the steps, triggering the spears to fly out of the sides of walls, but he deftly zooms out of the way and the spears clatter to the ground. When he reaches the bottom, he shifts back into his human form and takes a bow when I applaud his efforts.

Val just shakes her head and cautiously places a foot on the first step. When nothing happens, she takes another step and another. When it's obvious no more spears are forthcoming, she runs down to Khepri. He wraps her in his embrace.

Are they together? I wonder. My heart sinks at the thought.

Khepri holds up a hand to the line of prisoners. "You all wait here for a moment. We have a few more to rescue, before we make our grand escape," he commands.

"Do we have to wait too?" I ask Lover, disappointed that my best friend might leave me behind.

"Hell to the no," Lover responds and he and I jog to join the pair.

"Great job, Bestie," I commend Khepri, who just groans.

Maybe my veneration grates on his nerves? I'll have to reel it in.

Lover continues to light our path and I wonder if he's not a good friend, too, like Khepri—I decide to ask him.

"We can be," he answers, winking at me.

"What does that mean?" I whisper to Val.

"Honestly, I think it's more than you can handle right now," she says dryly.

"Ok," I agree, more to be amicable than from any real understanding. "Oh, look! Your friends!"

Up ahead, the end of the hall leads to a lonely jail cell, the only one in the vicinity. It is smaller and more cramped than other cells; it looks like it exists in complete darkness most of the time. In it are two people—*who, again, are vaguely familiar*. Maybe I've been in prison a long time, and that's why I know all these faces.

"I know you two!" I crow happily, then frown. "But, I can't remember your names. I'm Raiden," I announce proudly, excited that I remembered.

The one with goat legs and a furry tail poking out

underneath his ugly orange prison shirt looks questioningly at the others.

"Oh, Asteio! I'm so glad you're ok!" Val runs forward and puts her hands around the bars. The goat man walks forward, his tail wagging.

"You came!" he exclaims.

"Of course!"

She reaches between the bars and hugs him tightly. I wait patiently until she steps back and, then, take her place.

"Oh, Asteio! I'm so glad you're ok!" I parrot, hugging him to me.

Clearly, this man is one of our crew, and we've missed him. But perhaps he's not a big hugger, because he squirms in my grasp.

"Raiden's concussed," Val explains from behind me.

Asteio stops fighting my hold and starts to shake with laughter, while his cellmate practically chokes on his.

"And who is that?" I let go of our friend and point at his cellmate, a handsome Egyptian man with a dimple in his smile.

"He's the *Demigodling*," Khepri introduces, adding emphasis to his name. "And we've come to free him."

He must be pretty important—especially locked up like this.

Why, he must be the King of the gods!

I ask Khepri this thought and he nods in confirmation.

"I knew it!" I boast.

"Right, well, come on, King of the Gods and Furry Ass. We don't have much time," Khepri commands, and Val rushes back up to smash the bars with her hammer —*which is three times as big than before!*

"Wow! She has magical tools!" I blurt out.

"So do I," Lover says with an eyebrow waggle.

I give him a grin that feels a little silly on my face. I love these guys so much—and I love Asteio's nickname even more. *Furry Ass* suits him perfectly. I throw an arm around Lover and another around Val after she's decimated the cell. We watch the Demigodling exit first and, then, hold out a hand to escort Asteio through. He has true manners, that King of the Godlings.

"Let's get the fuck out of here," Khepri decrees.

"Yeah, let's blow this popsicle stand," she concurs.

"Let's leave this fuck hole," Tupac contributes.

We race back out the way we came. After we leave the spear stairwell behind and the conga-line of escaping prisoners (they've literally all decided to hold onto one another's shoulders and dance their way out) has rejoined us, Khepri leads us down a hidden hallway that reveals itself when he pushes on a stone in the wall.

We head down the secret passage and toward the exit, I presume, when Khepri yells at all of us to wait. He pushes past me to get in front and groans. I groan, too. Whatever is bad for my bestie is bad for me.

"A final trap," he spits out, fury lighting his dark blue eyes. "The Boats of Life."

"What are those?" Val asks.

"Basically, there are two boats. One leads to our escape—or to life. The other leads to ..."

"Our death," Val finishes for him.

"Except that Ra wouldn't give anyone a fifty-fifty chance of escaping," Khepri adds.

"So, they both lead to death," Lover growls.

"Son of a bitch," Furry Ass snarls.

"Son of a bitch!" I repeat because it feels right; then, I whisper to Asteio, "Who's Ra's mom? Is she that three-headed dog? What's its name?"

The King of the Gods doubles over in laughter. "This is fucking priceless," he finally manages to get out between his chortles.

"Did no one know Ra's mother was a bitch but Furry Ass?" I wonder.

The others join the Demigodling's enjoyment at learning this new fact. I do, too, because everyone needs a good laugh now and again.

"Ok, ok," Khepri gasps. "We've got to focus."

"Leave it to me," the King of the Gods announces before shifting into a massive bird with golden plumage and khol-lined eyes. He's so tall that his bird head is twice my height.

He gives a screech and then with one gigantic claw, he picks up Val and Asteio (aka Furry Ass). With the other, he wraps his talons around my bestie, Lover, and me.

With a mighty flap of his wings, he sets the boats racing forward. In the distance, a light appears—*the exit*!

I hear the rumble of stone and look up to see a stone wall descending high overhead. I realize that the brief glimpse of freedom is merely to taunt those in the boat. The wall ahead is about to come crashing down and the boats will crash into the rubble.

Luckily, we aren't in the boats. We are safely tucked away in the Demigodling's sharp hooks. Faster than lightning—and I know how fast that shit can be—the King of the Gods jets forward just as the wall comes crashing down above us.

The stones tumble toward my head and I hear them splash into the water behind us. I get drenched by the wave created by the fallen wall.

I sputter, spitting out the brackish water as the Demigodling sets all of us on the step just outside the exit door. Then, he transforms once more into his human form.

Val turns back to look at the wall. Before I can blink, she's raised her hammer and launched it through the air. It soars like an arrow, growing larger each second, until it's the size of a semi-truck when it crashes through the wall. It rips a circular hole through the wall.

I hear the other prisoners cheer loudly. The sound

of splashing reaches my ears and I know they've started swimming for the hole.

I smile, thinking this is over, and we've done it.

That's before I realize the semi-truck sized hammer is acting like a boomerang and hurtling right back toward us.

"Duck!" Asteio yells.

We all hit the floor.

The hammer smashes through the door and the wall surrounding the door, making a nice oversized exit.

"Mjoli, shrink! Please!" Val calls out.

I glance up from where I lay on my belly and I'll be a monkey's uncle if that hammer doesn't listen to her. It shrinks and lands gently in her palm.

Wait.

Am I a monkey's uncle?

I can't remember. I decide I'll ask one of the guys, but they are busy with other conversations.

"That was amazing. Thank you for saving our lives," Asteio says.

"Thank you for getting us out of there," Khepri adds. "The boats have been an issue I could not solve alone."

The Demigodling only shakes his head.

"I hope if any of us are in trouble in the future, you'll repay the favor," he counters.

"Always," I swear fervently. "I would do anything for my friends."

And I mean it—I would give my everything for Khepri, my bestie, and for the bewitching woman named Val. And Lover. And Furry Ass. And, of course, the King of the Gods.

Everything and anything.

11

VAL

I SKIP INTO THE BRIGHT SUNSHINE OF THE UNDERWORLD —it's night everywhere else—and skid to a halt. There, some twenty feet in front of the Butt Hole is *Dev*.

Holy-shit-I-swear-it's-true. Dev!

And that perfect man of my dreams is single-handedly manning my father's personal cart, where Tanny and Tangy are hitched.

I'm in awe.

Without even thinking, I run up to him, jump over the side into the cart and kiss him full on the lips. He stiffens under my assault, but I'm too overjoyed to really think about how far I am crossing the sexual assault line. I'm just so happy. So relieved. So overjoyed to see him. It's like the first time I ate Skittles. They were so overwhelmingly magnificent that I'd collapsed to my knees in the middle of the mall at age six and screamed, which Dot had laughed at me for a million times over the years. But the sight of Dev, there when I need him most, is just as magnificent as Skittles.

My lips move against his, relishing this moment and him.

To my surprise, he groans and begins kissing me back with equal ardor. His hands run sweetly over my arms and goosebumps raise under his touch.

Gods—how long have I yearned for this?

Forever, it seems like.

Before either of us can deepen the kiss like I secretly wish, I hear someone clear their throat in a very annoyed manner. I abruptly break apart from Dev, embarrassed at my wanton impulsiveness. I turn to find Lover staring daggers at Dev as he flicks his mullet over his shoulder. Bi-Polar looks torn between annoyance and amusement, but his attention is more fixed on Kung-Fu, who has grabbed his hand.

"Guys—this is Dev," I introduce, "He's come to help us get out of Duat!"

I can't believe this lucky break. Not only did Dev escape Asgard—*unscathed*—he somehow managed to find me and bring the exact thing we need to get everyone out of the underworld! Dad's cart can expand just like Mjoli, to fit as many people as necessary. (I may have been exposed to one too many drunken family dinner stories regaling an orgy that took place in the back of that wagon.)

I'm so happy that I could kiss Dev again, but I

refrain. His cheeks and ears are bright red and he's breathing pretty heavy ...

I think I definitely crossed a line.

Bad Val.

Very bad.

I'll have to apologize later, though, because I have my hands full. Lover doesn't look impressed with our human savior. In fact, he snorts when I introduce him, but I barrel on with my normal awkwardness.

"Dev, this is Lover—ah, not my lover, I mean ..."

"Well, we were intimate together."

My stomach drops out in horror. "You mean inmates? Cellmates?"

"Same difference," Lover shrugs, a smug look crossing his face as Dev takes a step back and swallows hard.

"No, it's not. We were inmates in the same cell—"

"We shared a bed," Lover offers.

Oh hell. I don't have time to argue with this delusional old man. I stare at Dev. "Not at the same time."

"She means not yet at the same time. She was on the bed, while I stood on the floor. Better angle," Lover says with a wink for me and a stink eye glare for Dev.

Holy fuck. I'm gonna have to slap that geezer. I ball my fists until Lover starts laughing. He slaps Dev on the back. "Don't worry. I love sharing. So long as I get to watch."

I roll my eyes upward and pray to Eir[1] for patience.

Dev's face now is entirely red and he looks furious.

ANN DENTON & MJ MARSTENS

"Don't talk about Val like that—she's a lady!" he snaps indignantly, affronted on my behalf. I've never seen Dev look so pissed.

I melt a little because he's so sweet, even though I'm not really offended. Gods are flirty by nature and this guy's been locked up for centuries; so, I really don't take Lover's words to heart.

Lover nods sagely.

"Like a 'lady in the streets and a freak in the sheets'?" he asks me with a suggestive wiggle of his eyebrows.

I burst into laughter, but Dev's glower only grows bigger and his face gets even redder. I'm a little concerned he might actually combust.

"Stop," I order Lover lightly.

"What? We both know that Purple Britches over there can't satisfy you—you need a real man."

I snort at his insinuation. "Yeah—I need a man, not someone old enough to be my great great grandfather," I retort.

"Oooooo," Bi-Polar taunts with a laugh, his wide shoulders shaking and drawing my eyes before I turn to see Lover frown.

By the look on Lover's face, he's settled for being amused by everything that's happening. He crosses his arms over his sculpted abs (definitely not grandpa abs there) and gives us all a smirk.

Dev, on the other hand, has taken Lover's words seriously.

"Purple Britches?!" he splutters incredulously.

"Yeah—what the fuck, dude? What grown-ass man actually wears lavender-colored pants?" Lover demands with a sneer.

"Well, at least I'm not wearing just underwear with a fucking sun stitched over the crotch to showcase my junk!" Dev snarls right back.

I'm a little startled by the savage fury evident in Dev's words and body language. I've never seen him so worked up before. Dev is always calm, cool, collected. I can't fathom why he's letting Lover upset him so much. But something about an angry Dev is twice as hot.

"You can't showcase your junk because you would need a fucking magnifying glass to see it!" Lover retorts and his arrogance and confidence are somehow attractive. Maybe that's because he combines his words with a couple of very precise pulses from his "sun."

Well, hello, Sunshine.

"Hey! Knock it off, you two!" I yell, trying to counteract their stupidity and my body's reactions to male caveman-esque showboating, but neither man listens to me. I look over to Bi-Polar, who just left Raiden in a corner of the cart and is now watching with a lazy smirk. "Are you going to help?!" I grit out.

He tips his head curiously at me.

"Help how? They don't need me to intervene. Besides, I think the bigger question here is why their fighting makes you so damn wet."

I swear to the gods I swallow my tongue and choke on it at his words. *Fuck. Busted.*

At least both Lover and Dev stop bickering, though.

"I'm not ... *that*," I deny in embarrassment. But as Khepri steps forward and his chest touches mine, just like it did before when he made me come in the prison hallway, I have to swallow hard. And I can't deny the catch in my breath, or how red my cheeks get.

Lover sniffs the air.

"You smell horny as fuck to me," Lover purrs in a deep voice that makes me even wetter.

I mean, if I were wet to begin with—because I'm totally not.

Lies.

I am.

I'm dripping like a leaky faucet of need, and not just for Dev. What's wrong with me?

I cringe.

"Guys, we need to get out of here," I remind everyone.

"She's right," Bi-Polar agrees. "We can talk about why fighting gets you off later."

Ugh.

Kill me now.

Behind us, the inmates are growing restless.

"This way, everyone!" I order, urging everyone towards the cart.

Dev looks apprehensive, but no one questions me and does as I've directed. Clearly, they know I have some tricks up my sleeve. Aside from having a magical hammer, I have a magical cart, too. Well—*my father does.* Like Mjölnir, the cart will stretch to accommodate the number of passengers and Tanny and Tangy never feel a weight change.

"Climb in!" I yell, "Quick! And don't touch the goats!"

Dev looks a little panicked as the cart begins to grow as more demis pour in. I join him at the helm.

"Thank you," I whisper for only him to hear.

I feel someone press up against my back.

"Don't thank me yet, princess," Lover whispers right back, clearly not caring that I wasn't talking to him.

I elbow him and Bi-Polar chuckles.

"Handy little chariot you have here, Fuck-Off," he compliments me.

"It is, isn't it? Bet you didn't think you could cram so many convicts into it, did you?" I joke.

"Makes me wonder what else you have that will stretch to accommodate lots of things," he teases right back.

"I have somethi—" Lover starts, but I cut him off before Dev can shove him over the edge.

"Tanny, Tangy—to freedom!" I shout and Dad's beloved goats take off.

I have no idea where freedom is, but Tanny and Tangy are smart. They'll know where to take us.

Hopefully, it's somewhere with a room where I can privately drown in my embarrassment.

DEV

I HAVE TO REMIND MYSELF THAT DEMIGODS CAN'T BE killed without magic. No matter how much I want to toss that Lover character overboard, I'm not going to be able to actually get rid of him. According to what Val's told me, he'd just be pissed and come back with a vengeance.

Per my massive amounts of research—aka listening to Val's stories about slights dating back to childhood and realizing she can't let go of the time her sisters called her Chicken Little for screaming that the sky was falling after she rode through a storm with her dad —demigods hold onto a grudge. Mullet man would probably survive the fall through the universe and find a way to haunt me with bad haircuts or something for the rest of my days.

I sigh and drop my annoyance at that Tiger King wannabe pressing against Val's side. She kissed me, I remind myself. And it was a fucking epic, way beyond friends type of kiss.

I let myself daydream of that as I hold the reins absently, not really doing anything as the goats pull us up above the clouds and navigate themselves, just like they did on the way here. Once I'd hitched up the cart, it was like they read my mind and knew what I wanted to do.

If this is Thor's job, he has it pretty good. Sit, back, relax, let the goats do the work for you and toss out a lightning bolt every now and again.

It kind of reminds me of my boss. I'm pretty sure he plays games on his phone most of the day, but every couple hours he'll stretch his legs and come peer over your shoulder, jolting you to attention.

As the cart lurches through the golden sky of Duat, I turn away from the horny bastard with yellow underwear and toward the Egyptian dude who looks like a guard standing on my left. I eye his outfit speculatively. There's not a lick of the prison-orange that Ra seems to have embraced with the other prisoners. Instead, this guy is wearing armor with a white sheet underneath, giving me a whole "Walk Like An Egyptian" vibe. Ra is fucking Egyptian. Suspicion makes the hairs on the back of my neck rise. What the hell is this guy doing here?

I move to stand between armor dude and Val, who can sometimes be too trusting. It makes me wonder what this guy might have said to get her to take him with us. He came in with some other dude who also wasn't dressed like a prisoner. Why are they here? Are they going to give these poor demis a taste of freedom then just wrench it away? Are we actually safe? Or is he one of Ra's lackeys? I reach into my pocket and finger the love arrow I still have in there. It's not much of a weapon, but it's the only one I've got. I tilt my head as I look into the Egyptian guard's kohl-lined blue eyes. "What were you in for?"

"I'm Khepri. I'm a guard. Or was."

Val leans over with a grin and pats Khepri's chest. "He helped us escape." She pulls back and leans on me almost like a girlfriend would.

My nerves sizzle like bacon.

Her touch is as delicious as bacon.

I might be hungry. I did skip dinner and technically go to hell and back (if Duat can count as hell) in order to help Val.

I give a wan smile in Khepri's direction and he extends a hand toward me. I still don't trust him completely. But I'll give him the benefit of the doubt. I push the reins over to my left hand so we can shake, my suspicion muted but not quite gone as he keeps talking.

"I'm a former sun god. Retired. Now, I'm just a god of shit." His grip is firm without being that dick-move intimidating, crush-your-bones type.

"By shit you mean …" I hope that's just a metaphor.

"Feces."

Gross. Ugh. I retract my hand and shove it in my pocket, wiping it off on the material inside and hoping he's not a 'hands on' kind of god. Why would he be a former sun god but keep the shit powers? It's one of those questions you can't ask out loud but will forever stick in your head when you look at a person, silently judging them.

Khepri grins like he knows what I'm doing, but he doesn't comment on it. Instead, he says, "Actually, I hate Ra. I only took this job to help the Demigodling escape. I knew every route out but never did think to steal another god's weapon. Or release everyone in order to cause enough chaos that my intended target could get away. That was all this beauty's idea."

I look down at said beauty and she smiles up at me.

Pride fills my chest. I've always known Val had so much more to give, and not just because she is part goddess—*because of her goodness*. I squeeze her against me again, before releasing her so she can turn and answer a question from one of the former prisoners.

I turn back to the front and look out. We trundle through Duat's sky until the yellow fades to the pitch black, diamond-scattered expanse of space. At first, I'm a little concerned about the whole death-by-suffocation-and-space-ice thing, but the cart does its magic thing and an invisible bonnet pops up over the sides that blurs my view a bit. We don't die, so it kind of feels like the supernatural equivalent of Oregon Trail. Actually, that's not true. If this was Oregon trail, the demis in this wagon would be dropping left and right from cholera and snake bites. Instead, behind us, Asteio is shooting wine through the air and a lot of pre-orgy action is happening. If Oregon Trail had looked anything like this, I would have been playing that game twenty four/seven instead of mocking my older brother for the fact that he liked retro computer games with subpar graphics.

I glance at a nymph who is currently naked and wrapping an arm that's transforming into a tree limb around the back of a guy with some deer antlers. When her nipple pops out of her top, I quickly turn forward again and next to me, the guard, Khepri, laughs. "Prudish?"

I hate how my neck and ears get flushed. It fucking sucks. "Orgies have never been my thing." That's a total lie. I love orgy porn. But you don't talk about that shit. That's the kind of secret you lie about to your significant other and take to the grave. Oh, and you make sure you've deleted all that crap long before you croak. Nothing sends a funeral straight to hell faster than your loved ones' discovery of your secret fetishes.

Khepri nods. "I can agree somewhat. Sex with complete strangers has never been as good. There needs to be chemistry. Your... girlfriend..." he trails off, clearly prying for more information.

My heartbeat quickens as he says the word I've wanted to assign to Val for years. But I just raise a brow. She'll have to define our relationship. I'm here for whatever it is. But I hope that kiss ... that jet-fueled, sonic boom of a kiss, is a sign that this Khepri dude is right.

He leans forward conspiratorially. "She's pretty sensitive, isn't she?"

My lips press into a thin line. This guy has already talked about smelling Val's desire. No way I'm going to talk with him in detail about Val in a sexual way, especially when I don't even know those answers myself. Soon. Soon. I hope. I cross every finger I've got. But though I hope to find out, I'm definitely not going to kiss and tell. So, instead, I change the subject.

"What exactly are your powers?" I ask.

His resulting grin is huge. "I'm so glad you asked." Khepri raises a tanned hand and snaps, his kohl-lined eyes crinkling at the edges in what could only be called an evil grin. Behind me, the demigod with the antlers shits his pants. And not just a little. We're talking trumpet-loud explosions that cause a lump in the back of his pants.

Dammit.

My eyes widen and I swallow hard. Thoughts of taking Khepri on disappear in a flash as the nymph woman tries desperately to disengage her tangled branches from deer-shit guy.

Khepri grins. "I'm not a huge fan of that guy. Most of the prisoners were in for bogus charges. Or because Ra hates them. But Aidan, son of Cernunnos[1] over there likes to chase maidens through the forest and rut them in beast form while they're still human."

I scrunch my eyes. "Don't a lot of gods do that?"

"Yeah, and if I could imprison all of them, I would. Those poor women are traumatized for life. I mean, just imagine being forced to make love to a bull, give birth to a baby minotaur, and then have to care for it.[2]"

I nod. "Good point." He's right. My pity for shitstain dissolves. Anger takes its place.

Khepri gestures out at the sea of prisoners. "On the other hand, most of these halflings are innocents. In particular, the Demigodling."

"What? Who?" I'm lost as my eyes scan over hundreds of people crowded into the back of the wagon.

The Egyptian god of shit points a tanned finger over at a bald guy who's currently making out with another dude with ... grey goat legs? Is that *Asteio*?

They break apart and I can see that it is. Both men are breathing heavily. Asteio's goat tail is wagging madly. And I definitely raise my line of sight so that I don't see if he's got a goat boner or not. There's no eyewash station on this wagon and I would definitely need one if I saw something like that. The goat dick. Not a guy dick. Guy on guy ... that's another one of those take it to the grave type of guilty pleasures.

Suddenly, I feel like an idiot for all those years I was secretly jealous, worried about Asteio's friendship with

Val. I'm an insecure jerkoff. I can admit it to myself at least.

I wave weakly at Asteio, who grins and does some finger guns in my direction, shooting wine right into my mouth and making me sputter.

"Shit, Asteio, warn a guy next time, will you?" I choke out. The wine that makes it into my mouth, and not onto my shirt, burns as it goes down. The ancients definitely have lower standards when it comes to alcohol than we do now. Asteio's wine tastes like rubbing alcohol.

Val leans around me and wags a hand at him. "Yeah, no choking my Dev."

Ah, shit. She called me hers. *Yes.* A little fire lights up in my chest. It crackles and jumps, sparks flying between us.

I swallow hard.

Damn. I still have a hard time believing she's staring up at me like that. Tenderly. My fucking heart is a rainbow-colored, cheesy-as-shit 1980s Lite-Brite. My head's a teenage girl with a side ponytail and scrunchie watching *Pretty in Pink* and swooning.

I want to kiss Val for an eternity.

Why does this moment have to be happening in front of a million other demis? I'm about to pluck Val off her feet and kiss her again despite the audience, but there's a beautiful Phillipino demigoddess wedging herself between us only seconds later.

Talk about a moment ruiner.

I have to contain my glare as she introduces herself.

"Hi, I'm Tala. And I'm not sure if you know this, but I can feel the sun hot on our trail."

I glance above us at the dark depths of space. I don't see anything but a ton of stars winking in the distance, and maybe a shadow that's a black hole. I definitely am not interested in finding out about that though. I'm just seconds into enjoying my existence completely and I'm not quite ready for it to end. I pull the reins slightly left so we give that sucker wide berth.

My eyes return to the petite woman with the serious expression.

"Excuse me?" I ask Tala, gesturing at the sky above our magical, transparent wagon bonnet, "but I think you might be mistaken. There's no sun near here."

The woman brushes her black hair backward and rolls her eyes at me. Of course she does. I'm just a puny human. Tala focuses her gaze on Val's grey-blue eyes. "My father is a sun god—"

I look over at the yellow-undie man with the sun on his crotch. "Is everyone's damn father a sun god?"

Asteio chuckles nearby and uses a goat hoof to paw the floor of the wagon. "There are a shit ton of sun gods, aren't there?"

Lover gives a shrug, drawing his long hair in back over one shoulder and then flexing his pecs in an alternating fashion, right then left. I'm not sure what that means, but I'm offended anyway.

Val shushes me, but then she puts an arm around

my waist before I can get upset by her actions. It's a smart move, because my brain basically starts to power off when her hand nears my right front pocket. It's the closest she's ever been to my dick and my body's suddenly overheating, picturing her hand sliding just a bit farther.

I try to look away and get myself under control, but that Khepri guy is there and he just smiles knowingly. If he can smell Val's orgasm, can he smell the fact that my cock is currently lubing up with precum just from a simple touch?

I hope not but I don't look at him because I don't want to find out. I let my eyes drift back over to Lover, whose gaze is narrowed on me and Val in what I assume is jealousy. Guess his tittie dance didn't get the reaction he wanted. Too bad. I pull Val harder against me. (Gods, it feels good to finally touch her the way I want.) I then try to tune in to whatever this Tala girl is saying.

"My dad is always trying to eat my mom and me," Tala explains, playing with the ends of her black hair.

My lip curls in disgust.

Lover steps forward until he's shoulder to shoulder with Val on the other side. Then he reaches out and taps Tala's shoulder. "Are you talking about ... incest?"

Tala sticks out her tongue. "Ew. Gross. No. Cannibalism. My mom tricked my dad into eating some of my siblings so now he's pissed and trying to eat us."[3]

"That's disappointing," Lover replies.

I'm not sure if he's disappointed by the lack of incest or the Silence of the Lambs style family dynamic. To me, both seem pretty damn horrific. I pull Val harder into my chest, glad that her father actually seems to love and care for her.

I can't help leaning down and placing a little kiss in her hair.

Val glances up at me with a soft smile that shoots right through my heart, piercing it more fully than any damn love arrow ever could. Her look only lasts a second before she turns back to Tala as the woman continues, "I can sense when my dad's coming for my family. I can feel him now. He's only a couple light years away. He must know that I've left the prison—"

"It's probably common knowledge by now," Khepri, the guard, interrupts. "Ra will know you all have escaped. He'll have spread the word."

Somehow, what was a minor conversation between Tala and Val, morphs into an address to everyone. When Khepri started to speak, a hush fell over all the demigods and stretched back across the wooden cart, which feels like it's currently the length of a football field, though I know that's a messed up exaggeration created by my imagination. The announcement about Ra cues a giant, 1950s style gasp from the crowd.

Then a chorus of squawks, curses, and worried shrieks go up.

"What are we going to do?"

"I can't let my mother find me! I just can't!" An

Indian god worries the ends of his handlebar mustache. He'd totally give off a Snidely Whiplash, cartoon-villain kind of vibe if he weren't hunch-shouldered and quaking right now. But, currently, he's not living up to his mustache's potential for evil.

(This is why I've never grown a mustache without a beard too. I can pull off a hippie look but I don't have enough badass evil villain in me to pull off a solo mustache.)

My contemplation is cut off by the panic surging through the demigods here who have more parental issues than the Lannisters from *Game of Thrones*.

"You're worried about your mother?" A tall woman with green skin yells at the mustache man. "My father wants to drink my blood to restore himself!"

Oh shit. The cart starts to waver as a panicked stampede forms and demigods rush around like headless chickens, bemoaning their impending doom. It does not help things when a comet streaks by.

I put two fingers to my mouth and give a loud-ass sports whistle, the only thing I actually learned from playing baseball for one season when I was nine.

The demigods all freeze and look at me. I look down at Val, who blinks. "Calm them down," I whisper.

It has to be her. They won't listen to me. She's the one who freed them. She has to take the lead here. I slide my hand down to give her a supportive tap on the back only to find that Lover's hand is back there, shoved into one of her jean pockets. He may or may not be kneading her ass.

I wanna punch that fucker then, but I restrain myself because this is Val's big moment. And I don't want to undermine her in front of her peers. And for some reason, she's letting him do that.

Does she think it's me?

Gods, I hope so. Partially because that would mean ass rubbing is on the table and partially because the thought of sharing her … ok, well, that goes in the hidden spank bank too—that thing is getting pretty full, I realize.

Val clears her throat and raises her voice. "Look, everyone, we're going to help you. I got you out, and I'm not going to just let your relatives entrap you again."

On my other side, Khepri takes a step forward. "I know most of you know me, and you may not believe me, but I have been working for centuries to find a way to help you out of that horror that Ra created. I have friends, Nut and Thoth, who will help hide you. I'm sure you've heard of Thoth, the Egyptian god of wisdom. He's been traveling throughout the multi-verses and afterlifes, helping hide demis for centuries."

I watch as skepticism and whispers roll through the cart like fog. These demigods don't believe any full god would help them. And I don't blame them. Based on what Val's told me, the divide between demis and full gods is almost worse than the divide between humans and gods, because demis are a threat.

Demis can steal a god's market share of worship. Demis can appear more relatable. They can give humans something to aspire to. Demis, like Val, can also be more lovable in a way that gods, say like the headless Hindu goddess[4] that I passed in the sky on my way to the prison, can't be. Sometimes the gods are just too intimidating. And it's easier to admire and praise someone who seems just a smidge better than you are, instead of ten times as fucked up.

I'm pretty sure I see one of the demis in the back of the wagon flip Khepri the bird. I'm about to step forward and speak up, vouching for Val's intentions, when the guy who was making out with Asteio steps forward.

The Demigodling.

"My mother trusts Khepri. You should as well." His voice is resonant in a way I don't expect, a way that has my heart calming and me taking an involuntary step toward him.

Khepri puts a hand on my shoulder. He turns me toward him and winks as all around us, the panic subsides and smiles slide back over people's faces.

This demigod has something. Charisma? Charm magic? Whatever it is—*I want it.*

Khepri leans in and whispers, "See why Ra didn't want him around? How can you compete with that?"

I nod. "I'm glad in my line of work, I don't have to."

Khepri laughs softly and asks what I do. I tell him as the Demigodling charms the pants (literally) off half the male gods in the room. Only Khepri, the dazed Japanese guard hunched in the corner, Lover, and I seem able to resist him. But I notice all our eyes keep darting toward Val.

I should feel possessive. I should want to fight them all. Or at least, I think I should feel that way. A normal human guy would feel that way.

But I'm not normal.

Neither is Val.

She's a goddess.

I notice her eyes do get stuck on the orgy several times and she bites that bottom lip in a way that makes me desperate. I notice Khepri and the Japanese guy sniffing hard in those moments. I wonder if he can smell her arousal even with all the other demis mixed in.

My thoughts are diverted when someone in the back of the wagon has a screaming orgasm and I make the mistake of looking dead on at the debauchery.

By the time we reach what Khepri claims is Nut's hiding spot, I'm more than ready for these writhing demigods to leave because I've discovered, while I like human orgy pornos, demigod spooge comes in every color, shape, and texture ... and not all of those are appealing to me. (A nymph whose cum is sawdust? Where she squirts and you think a chainsaw just bit into a tree? No. Uh-uh.)

I stare straight ahead, over the twitching ears of Val's goats, Tangy and … something else that starts with T. I've just started calling them TNT and singing the AC/DC song in my head to block out the grunts and strange noises going on behind me.

When the goats stop, it looks like we're at some kind of supernatural space station, with glass bubble buildings everywhere. It's not at all where I'd expect an Egyptian goddess to hang out. But then, I guess that's the point.

The goats roll to a stop in front of a building surrounded by turquoise bushes. They start nibbling on the blue-green leaves as Khepri turns and tells Val, "I'll just let Nut know we're here."

Then, to my shock, he transforms into a bug of some kind and flies off.

It feels like eons but is probably only minutes later when we get the demigods unloaded with a tall, lanky Egyptian woman who is wearing a pot on her head.

Once that's done, I expect us to turn in and bed down for the night. I'm really looking forward to the second half of that thought. Because I don't expect to be alone for once.

But Val turns to me and says, "We need to lead Ra away from all these demis. We have to give him a target to go after so they have a chance to hide."

"Target?" I ask, even though the stubborn set of her expression makes my heart sink.

"Yeah." She nods. "Me."

VAL

THE DEMIGODS ALL WAVE CHEERFUL GOODBYES TO US AS they disappear into the glass buildings ahead. Nut stands by the wagon, arm around the Demigodling's shoulders, with tears in her eyes. She promises to find Thoth, wherever he's currently hiding from Ra, so that he can help all these demigods find a place.

Asteio wants to go with us to help, but seeing as he's currently attached at the hip to the Demigodling, the one being Khepri sacrificed all to save, I shake my head.

The others do insist on coming with me, however. Khepri refuses to leave the wagon. "My fate is sealed," he says.

I suppose that means he knows Ra will find out that Khepri betrayed him. But the intense look in Khepri's blue eyes makes me swallow hard.

A tiny part of me wonders if he actually means something else.

Khepri just holds my gaze for a tension-filled moment, before he leads our willing hostage—Kung-Fu, the Japanese guard—into a corner of the wagon not coated in cum.

Lover, my short-term cellmate joins me and I'm less than surprised by this since he spent most of the wagon ride through time and space whispering sweet nothings in my ear—*I was shocked they were actually sweet.*

Whenever Dev wasn't looking, Tupac would lean over and say things like, "You hold a stormy sky in your eyes," or "Your skin is radiant in the starlight." Strangely enough, his odd old-fashioned compliments kind of made my heart do a little jump and click her heels together.

My heart's never done that for anyone but Dev.

Which makes me feel terribly guilty, so I shove the feeling aside and I try to rationalize it instead, with the fact that I think Lover just might be a little horny after all those years imprisoned—*the other demigods certainly were.*

Dev looked like he was about to die of embarrassment during the orgy. His ears turned fire-engine red at one point.

But for me, that just looked like a random Saturday night at my dad's house. I've always had to step around writing bodies if I wanted a midnight bowl of ice cream.

"Val, you came to my cell for a reason," Lover insists.

"Yeah, because that's where they put me," I tell him.

He shakes his head. "Nope. We're meant to be together."

I'm about to refuse when he follows that up with, "I'm meant to help you."

Because who can deny that I'm in over my head? Not me.

I did all this because it was wrong and I'm pissed. But underneath that, I don't have a plan for long-term escape from the sun god, Ra. I don't even know how I'm going to explain things to Dad. I doubt it's gonna be a cute "Lucy, you have some 'splaining to do," kind of moment.

"The one upside is that I'll probably never have to go to family dinner again," I mutter to myself.

"What's that?" Tupac leans closer, but I back away. I turn to dad's goats and let out a long, very specific, secret-code yodel.

Tangy and Tanny bleat once to show they understand. Then they bolt forward so fast that all of us fall back on our asses in the wagon—except for Raiden, who was already on his.

With a loud *shwook* we disappear from among all the stars and a pervasive darkness presses in on us. It almost feels suffocating.

Seconds later, with a *plop*, we appear in the night sky in the middle of a bunch of clouds.

Next to me, Dev clutches his heart. "What the hell was that?" he asks.

"Pop up storm," I reply, gesturing at the storm we manifested in order to jump back to the earthly realm. "It's the fastest way to get around."

He just nods as he tries to fight off a heart attack. I bite my lip as I stare at him. "Dev, can we hide out at your place for a bit?" I swallow hard. "I hate to ask, but we probably could all use an hour or two of sleep before we—"

"Of course."

That selflessness that I love about him overcomes his fear.

I smile at him and he smiles at me until the goats, having overheard our conversation, take off and we fall back on our elbows.

Mine lands in some gooey substance and I cringe. I definitely don't want to know what it is, but I can guess.

Thankfully, seconds later, we're all piling out of the wagon onto Devin's roof. Surreptitiously, I rub my elbows clean on the side of the cart.

Khepri holds out a hand for Kung-Fu to take so he can help him up.

Raiden beams an adoring smile up at him. "Thanks, Bestie!" he tells Bi-Polar in an odd, euphoric manner.

Someone definitely doesn't have their memory back

yet—*and I freaking shudder to think about what the guard will be like when he does recover.*

Tupac rushes ahead to open the door for me and I have to bite down on a smile. He's weirdly romantic.

Dev takes my hand again as we descend the dim stairwell and once we're in the dark, touching, my breath hitches. I still can't believe I kissed him. My mind whirls with awe and desperate worry. He's here, he's with me ... but I've also put him in danger.

The gods will be after him—*and it's all my fault.*

Dev unlocks his door and lets us in.

"Are those hemp plants?" Tupac walks in and goes straight for them. "We used to farm these regularly after the Spanish arrived."

Dev nods and pulls me aside as Khepri enters with Raiden, who has his arms slung around the Egyptian guard in full-on comradery.

"Why don't you both sit down," I suggest because I can see Kung-Fu's newfound friendship with Khepri is wearing on Bi-Polar.

Khepri carelessly shoves Raiden toward the couch and, then, shuts and locks the door. "I'm going to do a perimeter check of this space. See if I can smell anything." He shifts into a beetle and buzzes off.

Dev pulls me with him over to the fridge and grabs a six pack of beer. He sets it on the counter.

"I think we need a drink," he states.

"I think we need a toast, to the most magnificent

demigoddess ever to exist," Tupac grabs a beer and holds it up in my direction.

I flush as he and Dev both level me with admiring looks. My eyes drop and my cheeks grow warm, but so does the inside of my chest. My impulsive, rather pissed-off plan worked—for now—who would have thought?

"We still need to figure out how to elude Ra," I mention. This battle is far from won.

"We will," Tupac takes a huge drink and then studies the golden oak cupboards. "What kind of food do you have?"

"I dunno; take a look and help yourself." Dev pulls me out of the kitchen and into the dining room just as Khepri reappears in the kitchen and resumes his human form.

"All clear," the Egyptian guard declares.

"Great. Well, mi casa es su casa and all that jazz. One of you can take the bedroom on that side," Dev gestures to the door next to the kitchen. "And one of you can take the couch. Val and I are gonna go crash." He tries to sound casual but his hand crushes mine.

My nipples tighten as I realize what this means. Me and Dev. Dev and me. In his room. Together.

Yes.

I look up at Dev's brown eyes and see they're dark with urgency. My core tightens. We need to get out of here before Khepri or Raiden can smell my arousal.

I yank Dev down the hallway, ignoring Tupac's

questions about some of the items in the fridge. He'll figure modern, non-prison food out.

I have more important things to address—namely, why Dev and I are still wearing clothes.

I shove open the door to his bedroom. I've already been here plenty of times—though he doesn't know it.

I shove the door shut behind us and immediately strip off my prison issue sweatshirt, my boots, daisy dukes, and crop top. I'm naked in under ten seconds.

Dev gasps as his eyes roam down my figure.

And then I get nervous. Because he's still completely dressed. "Fuck. Did you mean actually sleep?"

In response, Dev crashes into me, arms going around my waist and pulling me into him. His lips find mine and he places an aggressive, very un-Dev-like kiss on my lips as he lifts me up. He walks me to the bed and sets me gently on the edge before pulling back from our kiss.

"Not at all. I'm gonna crash into you so hard you'll be limper than a test dummy."

I giggle at the very unsexy and unromantic analogy, but that giggle quickly turns into a moan as his lips roam down my chest and latch onto a nipple. His fingers come up and play with my slit and I'm so glad I waxed a week ago.

Heat travels up my spine and sensation flickers across my nerves like sparkling glitter.

"I've wanted this for so long," Dev admits.

Hearing that just takes my desire up a notch.

His talented fingers kick it up further as they circle my slick center.

"I've wanted you since the moment I saw you," Dev confesses.

"Me too," I admit as his fingers make me start to buck.

His tongue sneaks out and he laps at my nipple, using the same rhythm on it as his fingers use on my clit. They go faster and faster until I explode, my hands flying down to clamp Dev's head in place as I writhe against his mouth.

When I come down, he just repeats the process until I am as limp-limbed as he claimed he'd make me.

I don't even stir when I hear a thump in the living room.

Dev's head whips to the side. He's still fully clothed, and the look on his face says he wants to go investigate, but I wrap my legs around him and draw him in. "No, please—*don't go!* Those three can fend for themselves and I *need* you, Dev. We've waited too long."

My chest tightens and grows fluttery and bubbly as Dev slowly removes his shirt. He reveals the toned abs and pecs I'd always seen hinted at under his clothes before but never fully shown to me. I can't resist, I have to lean up to drag my hands over him. And a confession leaks out my lips. "I used my spare key all the time to sneak in here and make myself come on your bed," I tell him.

He groans and shoves me back as he makes quick work of his pants and then climbs over me.

"Tell me about it," he whispers as he spreads my thighs apart and traces over my entrance with his cock.

"I used to lay on your pillow, so I could smell it while I fingered myself. I'd pretend you'd just gotten out of bed and were in the shower or something, and I needed to get myself ready for you before you got out so I could convince you to fuck me before you went to work."

He moans and nips at my bottom lip. "Show me," he commands, pulling back.

I slide my fingers down my chest to my wet slit and lubricate them before I start circling my clit.

Dev watches me with hooded eyes for a few seconds before he moans and says, "I can't wait." He pushes my hand aside and sheathes himself in me, sliding slowly in before rolling us sideways so that he ends up on bottom and I end up on top. His fingers creep up to tweak my nipples.

Damn. My fists curl and I reach forward to grab his bed frame so that I don't hurt him. The orgasm that's building inside me is intense.

I swivel my hips and his dick hits the perfect spot as I grind my clit down on him. I don't stop moving even as my body begins to shudder. My fingers clench and I accidentally break off the top piece of the headboard as I climax.

"Fuck!" I cry, holding the wood aloft so I don't hurt Dev even as stars flicker behind my eyelids.

"Holy shit," he cries, and I'm not sure if it's because of how right we feel together or because I accidentally mutilated his bed.

I don't ask, I keep grinding, headboard in my hands, until my orgasm subsides.

That's when I throw the piece of mutilated wood to the side—*only to spot Tupac sitting in Dev's armchair in the corner of the bedroom.* He's pulled the chair closer to the bed and is sitting there with a bowl of popcorn in his lap, enjoying the show.

I give him an incredulous look, even as Dev, who hasn't noticed him, pumps up into me.

Tupac stares at us as he eats another piece of popcorn. "Don't stop. Keep going. It's like watching Twilight in reverse. I loved Twilight."

Dev throws a pillow at him and then, to my surprise, flips us so that he's on top—*totally reclaiming his masculinity with the smooth move.* And all my fear about hurting Dev flies out the window as he begins to pound me—*hard.* His dick slams so deep into me that he hits my cervix. His hands reach down and encase my breasts and he tweaks my nipples as his hip bones smack against mine and make my entire body ripple with pleasure.

I gasp mindlessly, the moans tripping and escaping my lips as Dev pushes me higher and higher.

From his chair, Lover gives a breathy, "Oh yes."

For some reason, his voyeurism just makes all of this hotter. But I don't look at him. This is about Dev and me. This is our first time. And it's precious.

I stare up into his eyes and my own start to blur even as he rails me.

As soon as he notices that, he slows. "Val, did I hurt—"

I lean up and grab the back of his neck. I cut him off with a kiss. A hard brutal kiss, but I'm past holding back with him. *I love him.*

He pumps again as our mouths nip and bite and suck ravenously at one another's lips and his hands roam down the sheets and start to knead my ass. And then his dick hits that spot—*that perfect spot.*

I shatter like I'm made of glass.

Dev comes only seconds later and my heart swells even more to watch his face tilt toward the sky as he pumps into me.

When he's done, he looks down at me with a soft smile that quickly morphs into a horrified expression. "Fuck. I came inside you."

I rub his arm. "Don't worry. It's fine. It's not the right time of the month or anything. I just lose my immortality if I'm not a virgin."

Dev slides back, his dick popping out of me. Color drains from his face. "What?" His hand scrubs over his beard. "So, now Ra can now kill you? Because of me?"

I lean forward and trace up his chest, tweaking a nipple. "Dev, shut up. I was jok—"

But he's shaking his head and turning to Tupac, who's sliding his own limp dick back into his yellow undies with a hand covered in cum. His popcorn bowl sits on the floor beside him.

"Can you help protect her?" Dev asks harshly.

"I can wear a condom, but I'm not a huge fan—"

"Not like that, you dick! Her life! Can you protect her *life*?"

The demigod nods. "It's what cellmates do."

I only focus on Dev's relief for a second as he turns back and kisses me tenderly, running a hand down the side of my neck like I'm the most precious thing in the world to him.

But then my brain catches up with my ears. I turn to ask Tupac, "Did you say cell mates? Or *soulmates*?"

But the voyeuristic demigod has disappeared.

I turn back to Dev with worried eyes.

But all I see is gentle acceptance. Dev uses his hand to trace over my lip. "No matter what he said, you need him, Val." He leans forward and places a gentle kiss on the tip of my nose. "You need the other guys, too."

"But ..." *Is he saying what I think he might be saying?* No. He can't be. Humans are monogamous. They are one and done. They aren't like gods ...

I must have spoken aloud because Dev leans over so his face is aligned with mine. "You're not fully human Val. I get it. And you have different needs."

"But you ..."

His face turns sober. "I need you to stay alive. That's it. End of story."

"But …" I still can't believe he's okay with this.

Dev grins and gives me a light tap on the ass. "Maybe next time, I'll bring the popcorn."

KHEPRI

THE SCENT OF VAL'S ORGASMS FILLS THE APARTMENT with delicious temptation, like waffles covered in butter and maple syrup. I inhale and sigh. One day, I want to taste one of those orgasms.

Raiden gazes up at me from the floor (because I kicked him off the couch) with a puppy-like expression in his eyes. "Do we get to go next?" he asks.

"Duat, I hope so," I tell him.

He babbles happily after that and plays with a little bit of lightning between his fingertips. I almost feel sorry for the prick. Almost. I wouldn't want to be caught and concussedly stupid around my worst enemies.

When Raiden starts to use his own lighting on his tongue and giggle, that's when I can't stand it anymore. I call down the hall, "You done in there? Or accepting visitors?"

Devin comes out into the hall, still buttoning up the top button of his collared shirt. I don't think I've seen an expression on his face other than sheepish since the moment I met him.

Behind him stumbles Val, who takes his hand, looking giggly and edible. Her cheeks are flushed and even with her bra on, her nipples are still pebbled. "We better go check on the goats or they might start gnawing on your neighbors satellite dishes," she tells Devin before glancing up at me.

Her cheeks grow red when she sees the look in my eyes and remembers my keen sense of smell.

I follow the two of them to the door and Raiden bumps into my shoulder just as we're about to leave. "Me too!" he exclaims.

I turn to push him behind me, where he belongs, only to see Tupac strolling out of Devin's bedroom with a popcorn dish in hand and dried cum on the side of his yellow underpants. (I know it's cum because I can smell it.)

My jaw drops and fury heats me more than the sun on my shoulders ever did. "You were in there!" Was he participating?! I might officially hate someone else in the universe as much as Ra. Devin and Val, well anyone could see that writing on the wall, but him?

Tupac sets down his popcorn bowl on the dining table and strides to the door. He tries to squeeze past me but I block him in. I lean forward into his face. "What the hell?"

"Relax. I was just watching. This time." He winks before he squeezes past me. He sprints down the hallway to catch up with Val and Dev, calling out, "Wait! Let me escort you, beautiful lady."

"We could have watched?" Raiden says from my side.

I smack him across the side of the head. But it's not really him that I'm mad at. I stomp down the hall after everyone else. I could have fucking watched. And I hadn't even known it.

Godsdamned motherfucking honor.

We reach the roof and my bitterness is shattered when an ear-piercing shriek fills the air. Soon, dozens of the same shrill cry sound in the distance. The sounds are faint to me but I see Dev clap both hands over his head and fall to his knees. The goats bleat angrily behind them.

Raiden, Tupac and I look to the sky where dark clouds obscure our view, but Val rushes over to her human lover, throwing her body over his.

"Quick! Tupac, get him to protection!" Val yells.

"What's going on?" I demand.

"Valkyries are coming," she announces, her lips thinning.

The Incan solar deity doesn't need to be told twice. He rushes forward as Val steps back. Then he uses his bulging arms to yank Dev up and run swiftly in the opposite direction of the racket.

"Valkyries, you say?" I ask almost conversationally,

although all my muscles are tensed for impending attack.

"I mean, technically, my sisters."

"Hmm, maybe they are just coming to chat?" Raiden suggests.

Oh, humans, I can't wait for his brain to get better. Idiot Raiden is worse than regular Raiden.

"They hate my guts," Val admits ruefully.

"I bet holidays are interesting," I joke, trying to break the tension, though my eyes still scan the sky.

Val laughs. "Try our weekly family dinners … in fact, I'm pretty sure that's why my big *sissies* are paying me a call."

"Does this have anything to do with why you were imprisoned?" I wonder. We typically don't see charges until months after lock up. Ra doesn't feel any need to be efficient since there is no such thing as a true appeals process.

"It has everything to do with why I was put in the Back Hole!" she announces cheerfully.

"Black Hole," Raiden corrects. "It has an L." He starts to say "la la la" as if he's trying to teach Val to say the letter 'L' and I roll my eyes before glancing back at the sky.

The shrieks, which were faint, have doubled in volume and I now see a couple of shadows circling in the clouds above like vultures.

An ominous feeling creeps over me, even though

I'm immortal. Something primal even affects gods when they feel like they are hunted. "Who cares!" I interject, gesturing above us. "Why are the "Angels of Death" descending upon us?!"

Val winces at my accurate description of her and her sisters.

"BecauseIgaveeveryonetheshits," she says in a rush.

"What?" Raiden and I both exclaim, and I nearly forget about the looming airstrike.

Did she just say shits?

As in, *my* power?

As in, *the most gloriously underlooked regenerative power in all creation*?

My dick pulses.

"Can we talk about this later?" she huffs just as the sky is filled with golden-haired maidens with glorious wings.

Leading the Valkyries, though, are two women that are definitely not the same as the others. They are riding in a horse-drawn chariot. Clouds disintegrate as they burst through them so that they become backlit by a weak sun. Their battle-gear gleams.

"Who the hell are they?" I ask.

"Sif and Járnsaxa, my father's wife and consort," she answers casually. "Really, after all the years of spiteful bickering between the two of them, you would think my father would rejoice that I gave them a reason to unite."

"And what are their powers?" I demand.

"Aside from being petty cuntcushions? Well, Sif can make wheat grow like crazy and blow up her boobs to the size of watermelons. Járnsaxa ... doesn't really do much."

"Petty cuntcushions?" I arch a brow. "Creative."

Val shrugs.

"I read it in a book once. Venus—or Aphrodite—was way cooler in that book than in real life, let me tell you."

I snort, staring at the women in the sky who have paused their advance.

"What are they waiting for?" I wonder.

"I dunno. Maybe an invitation to engage?" Val offers. "They are super stupid and super into protocol. Since I've never battled before and I never really listened to Dad's old war stories, I have no idea."

"They're planning their attack," Raiden announces.

He can't be right. Those women cannot literally be paused in the sky like some Macy's Day Parade blimp waiting for horse shit to be cleaned off the road in front of them. *No.* It has to be the concussion talking. He has to be wrong, but Val's stepmoms and sisters keep pointing.

"Don't you plan this shit *beforehand*?" I point out.

Val retorts, "I just said they were dumb. And slutty. They're more likely to engage you in sex acts than acts of war. Actually, that pisses me off more—they better fucking not!" she snaps angrily.

I throw a startled glance at Raiden, but he's struggling to pull his guard-issued sword out of his scabbard. His fingers keep slipping.

"My hands don't work. My hands don't work," he mutters in mild panic.

"Trust me—I'm not going to fuck your slutty, dumb family members," I reassure Val distractedly.

"Nor I," Raiden concurs, though his statement is punctuated by a clatter when he drops his sword, which makes me want to face palm on his behalf.

"Good. Because I'm pretty sure they have godly chlamydia or something," Val says with a grimace, making me chuckle.

"Should I just electrocute them?" Raiden offers, fingers crackling.

Out of everything, his lightning power seems to be the only thing still functioning properly.

"Nah, don't waste your time. My sisters are immune to it and are protecting my stepmoms, no doubt. The worst it will do to them is give them a bad hair day—although, that would piss them off. Their blonde hair is their pride and joy," Val says with an animosity that I pick up on.

The Japanese god rests a hand briefly on her shoulder.

"I've always liked the brune—brune—brune... brown hairs," he tells her solemnly, putting a fist to his chest.

"I like 'em when the carpet matches the drapes," I

throw in with an eyebrow waggle as I put my own fist to my chest and mock him. Raiden scowls at me and Val giggles and rolls her eyes.

"This is serious," Raiden the Cumstain scowls at me.

"I know," I agree mockingly, about to laugh because he looks like an angry two-year-old. "Can you imagine if the Valkyries' pubes match their hair? We can get our braid on."

"Oh, gods, that's so disturbing. And can you please focus?" Val's temper flares. "Tupac's shielding Dev, but I really don't want to have to strangle one of my sisters because something happened to him. Dad would be pretty pissed at me—he loves all his kids, no matter how stupid or skanky."

I glance up at the hovering chariot, where the two women are now yelling at one another so obnoxiously that even the Valkyries who surround them look annoyed and have crossed their arms as they hover in the dark clouds, awaiting orders.

"Want me to turn into a monkey and throw chunks of shit at them?" I propose.

"You can do that?" Val asks at the same time Raiden growls, "No."

"Well, what do you suggest, O Honorable One?" I parry back to the unhelpful Japanese dick.

At least Val seemed impressed with my crappy idea.

"Maybe I can drown them a little? You know, make a mini-monsoon or something." Raiden holds up a finger and a tiny disappointing jet of water squirts from it, like his finger is one of those Dollar Store squirt guns that are painted so bright and enticingly but do not smite your enemies the way their coloring promises. (I have quite horrific memories of last year's Egyptian pantheon reunion, where I was in charge of the games for the afternoon.)

"Dammit," Raiden growls and blows a raspberry at his own finger.

Suddenly, one of the figures in the chariot holds up something that glows.

"Whoa. Wait! What is Bitchmom Two holding?"

Val squints up at the sky.

"You mean Járnsaxa? She looks like she's got … a lightning bolt? Dad doesn't make those."

"No," I frown. "Zeus does." Well, fuck—I guess they came with back-up after all.

"Uh-oh. That's strong shit." Raiden's hand flops over his mouth with a pop. "The good news is they can't hurt me."

My nostrils flare and my lips thin, though I'm not certain if Raiden's being a dick on purpose right now or if he's still affected by the hammer.

When he adds, "But you better watch out. Better not shout. They can hurt you and that panty-wearing prisoner," Raiden says, pointing over at Tupac, A.K.A Sunny, A.K.A Lover, where the Aztec demi is trying to convince Dev to go into the door that leads to the apartments—but Dev's fighting him and doing a pretty decent job of it.

"Tupac," Val says absently, nibbling her lip in worry as she stares overhead. "His name isn't prisoner. What are we going to do?! I have never been in a battle. The closest thing I've been in is a cardio kickboxing class."

"Well, both the Valkyries and the lightning bolts can kill Dev, so he probably needs to go inside." I scold loudly, so that the human will stop fighting against Tupac's hold.

From across the roof, Tupac calls out in a stage whisper, "Valkyries who aren't virgins are also mortal, *hint hint.*"

Fuck. That means these idiots could kill Val. I pull her in closer and wrap my arm around her as I glare up at the sky.

"Well, none of my sisters are virgins either," she adds. "So those bitches are just as mortal as I am."

I look at Raiden. It seems like I have no choice but to work with him. "Since they really can't hurt you, we'll try to get Járnsaxa and Sif to throw all those bolts at you."

"Yeah, ok. Get struck by lightning. Good plan," Raiden agrees, not an ounce of sarcasm in his tone.

"The stingy bastard won't have given them many bolts," I pat his back. "I'm sure you'll be fine. I'll just stay out of the way until then, I guess, but I'm prepared for when shit hits the fan—poop pun intended."

Raiden stomps forward and starts waving his arms.

"Magnificent sky pretties," he yells, addressing the

two women leading the pack, "to what do we owe the honor of your presence?"

He biffed that big time. Both Val and I choke at his words but, instantly, the two women seem mollified. They really are idiots.

"We want the abomination standing behind you," Sif demands imperiously.

"Please, take him. He's a real pain in the ass," Raiden deadpans and I realize the fucker is referring to me even though it was obvious that Sif meant Val. My eyes narrow and I glare at him, wondering just how stupid he still is.

Járnsaxa looks confused—but she seems like the type that struggles to breathe and walk at the same time. I mutter this under my breath, making Val's tinkling laugh ring out. Sif's face darkens with anger at the sound of Val's chuckle and I instinctively try to shove her behind me but Val isn't having any of it.

"Don't be stupid," she hisses. "I can take a Zeus bolt to the heart, but it might incapacitate you —*permanently.*"

"Firstly," I hiss right back, "that's highly unlikely. I'm *very* hard to kill—more so than the majority of the gods. Secondly, you should say 'don't be Járnsaxa.' It has a better ring to it than 'don't be stupid.' Actually, I've been calling her Bitchmom Two in my head," I confess, earning me another coveted grin from my Nordic brunette beauty.

"I like it. Now, stand back," she commands before

ANN DENTON & MJ MARSTENS

stepping next to Raiden. "I am not an abomination," she yells to the Heavens. "I'm a person—just like all of you—and just as worthy. All my life, you've treated me as a second-rate family member and I'm sick of it. Go away and grow up. What my father sees in all of you, I'll never know. He clearly inherited grandfather's blind eye[1] where you all are concerned."

All the women above us gasp—I assume they're gasping about the slur on the great Odin, but who knows how these spineless and brainless twats think—and, *finally*, the attack begins.

Why they waited so long, is beyond me, but they aren't the brightest lightning bolts in the sky.

At least their aim is better. Bitchmom One and Two throw four of Zeus' bolts directly at Val. Each one zaps down faster than I can blink, hitting their mark and lighting Val up like a Tesla coil.

Although they don't do any permanent damage, I can see by Val's wince that they are still uncomfortable and fury fills my being. Raiden's face goes positively livid at the sight of Val's pain and he steps in front of her and unleashes his thunderous wrath.

The empty look in his eyes fades a little as the ground trembles beneath his rage, the winds pick up, and rain begins to pelt everything and everyone.

"Leave her alone," he intones in a voice so deep and rumbling that even I quell a little at the sound, "or else."

"Or else what?" Val asks, sounding genuinely

curious and I almost laugh when Raiden rubs two fingers to his temple in exasperation.

"Will you just let me handle this?" he demands, only to be struck by three of Zeus' thunderbolts next.

Like Val, his face is etched with agony but, unlike Val, he drops to his knees. I raise a brow at my Nordic demi-goddess. This girl is *tough*. Though he's a full god and she's only half, the worship levels for Thor and Zeus are much higher. It makes me wonder if Val's honestly more powerful than Raiden. Which is not good for us. Not good at all. Because she doesn't have any manifest powers. She can't attack. If Raiden's weaker than these thunderbolts, we might be in trouble.

Too late, I realize that the Valkyries are swooping in, brandishing various weapons that—while they may not kill any of us but Dev—will hurt like a mother-fucker. I quickly form two lumps of Number Two in my hands and warily watch one blond bitch descend upon me with *a freaking ax*.

Yeah, my ass already has a crack—it doesn't need two—and, certainly, no other body part of mine is looking to be cleaved in half.

She zooms at me like an angry bird and swings the blade at my throat. I duck and rise up in time to smash one shit-imbued palm into her face. She screeches inhumanly when the stench fills her nostrils—which was Járnsaxa of her because, now, it's in her mouth—

155

and flaps frantically around midair, spitting more than Daffy Duck.

Everyone else seems to freeze and watch her struggle and I seriously begin to doubt the powers of the Valkyries on a battlefield. They're like cats on the hunt until someone flashes a light and teases them for hours as they try to catch it. Ax-Slut finally manages to scrape enough dookie off her face to point a trembling finger at me.

"Get him!" she screams and, instantly, all the ladies turn their attention toward me—and *not* in the sexy good way. More in the 'let's see if we can kill a fellow god today' way.

Very disappointing.

Bitchmom One and Two grab the remaining lightning bolts and throw them at me. Those fuckers fly through the sky as fast as fishing spears and I briefly turn into my dung beetle to avoid them.

I successfully dodge three bolts. I change back into my human form in order to avoid a Valkyrie who attempts to smash me between her palms.

Too late, I can see myself spinning into the fourth and final one. The world suddenly becomes exceedingly slow as I watch the electric point get closer and closer to my heart. Well fuck.

There's absolutely no time for me to dodge it.

So I do the one last thing I want to do in this life, look at Val.

To my left, I see her sucker punch one of her cunt

sisters and I wish that she had a handful of shit when she did it.

That would have been a thing of beauty.

She turns in horror to see what's about to happen to me and lunges. Val throws herself bodily into me, even as I shake my head, telling her it's too late.

She flaps her arms uselessly, like they might give her added speed and, to my surprise, *they transform into white wings*. The rest of her body follows suit. Her neck elongates and legs shorten and in a golden glow, she changes form. Where there once was a woman now flies a magnificent swan.

Holy shit (yes, it's holy).

Just in time, Val dives in front of me and fucking *swallows* the lightning bolt.

Instantly, she falls to the ground.

I lean over her, fear for her worse than any fear I've ever felt for myself. I run my hand across one of her delicate white wings and whisper, "Val?"

I'm afraid that her asshole sisters and stepmoms actually killed her. The goats must feel the same because they start thrashing and bucking, trying to kick the cart away and get to her.

But, to my relief, Val the Swan suddenly squawks back to life in a flurry of flapping wings and angry honks, and every time she opens her mouth—orange lightning streaks forth.

I feel a satisfied smile stretch my face as the electricity arcs from her beak into one of the crazy vapid women above us. The one with the ax who tried to cleave me in half like a bad magician. And unlike Raiden's powers, Val's lightning fucking burns the hair off that sky bitch. She falls, shrieking and crying as her blond locks are eaten away by orange lightning.

All I can think is that it's raining stupidity today.

15

VAL

ONE SECOND I'M A PERFECTLY NORMAL POWERLESS demi-goddess; the next, I'm a freaking swan who breathes lightning—*like some kind of seriously messed up, but badass dragon.*

All my life, I've wished I had powers like everyone else in my family and, now that I've got them, I'm not quite sure what to make of them. I mean, a swan? Really?

At first glance, my powers seem pretty ... well, *useless*; that is, until I bark out an orange lightning bolt at Sif and Járnsaxa and watch in fascination as they seize and quake in their chariot and, then, tunk over, their heads disappearing from view.

I feel my swan brows raise in surprise—my step-moms aren't immune to my lightning powers. And my sisters ... while immune, can still clearly get their hair burnt to a crisp.

I feel my beak curve into a victorious grin—which sounds super creepy. I'm half-intrigued, half-disturbed by the thought of what I must look like, but turn my attention to my remaining half-sisters. It's time for a little payback and I've heard it's a bitch. I chuckle internally at my dumb inner monologue as I chase the witless whores who've spent years making me miserable.

I shoot up through the sky, and though I've never flown before, I somehow know exactly what to do. The air currents shove me up exactly where I need to be, so that I'm level with those black winged hoes.

Raiden shoots an extra blast of air toward me and I rush forward. He's literally the wind beneath my wings.

My stepsisters scatter like flies.

Every few seconds, I honk and shoot my electric power through their bodies and watch everything from their eyelashes to eyebrows to beautiful blond curls turn to ash and scatter behind them, leaving bald heads. The smell is horrific, but luckily, my swan beak is less sensitive than my human nose.

I'm delighted to discover that many of these Valkyries cannot rock the bald look as their skulls are not fully symmetrical. And I just love that they're gonna have to go home looking like this. My goose mouth lets out a long, wavering laugh honk.

It doesn't take long before every last one is bald and flying for cover. I wing-pump the air in victory—until I hear Tupac shouting for help.

No!

Swiftly, I turn to fly over to him, but my long neck overshoots, and I end up spinning a circle. Whoever said swans are innately graceful never counted on me becoming one, that's for sure.

When I finally manage to regain my equilibrium, I zoom through the air toward Dev and Tupac, who are surrounded by *jackals*.

Tan dogs with pointed noses, grey fur striping their spine, and huge pointed ears, they bare their teeth and prowl closer. Shit! I don't know much about Egyptian deities but I do remember something about jackals and the land of the dead.

I push my wings faster.

Raiden is attempting to waterboard one of my sisters (mostly succeeding in spraying her at random moments) while it looks like Khepri is mud wrestling another. Only, that isn't mud. Either way, I'm going to be the first to get to Tupac and Devin who are being backed into a corner of the roof, one without a ledge.

Khepri notices the jackals when his opponent slips and falls, getting shit-faced. "Dammit all to Duat," he swears at the sight of the dogs and mutters something about Ra sending reinforcements.

I shoot him a birdy sideways glance. Ra's just sending reinforcements *now*? This seriously has to be the world's most uncoordinated attack *ever*.

But I backtrack on that thought as my eyes narrow and I try to pinpoint which jackal is the alpha dog. It's much more likely that my stepmoms and sisters fucked up and started their attack too soon ... *which would explain why they waited so long to do anything.*

Any other time, this would be hilarious.

But, I'm not laughing right now—partly because I'm a swan, but mostly because Ra's *dogs* are threatening *my* men. I mean my Dev—*Lover isn't mine ...*

I ignore the errant thought as I, yet again, race to save my friends.

But Tupac proves he's more than just jokes and innuendos. With an easy flick of his wrist, a freaking ring of fire surrounds him and Dev. The one closest to them yips and jumps back. And though they pace the perimeter, the golden flames sufficiently keep the wild dogs at bay. I swear that over the roar of the fire, I can hear Tupac singing ...

"Love is a burning thing, and it makes a fiery ring. Bound by wild desire, I fell into a ring of fire."

Raiden is shaking his head, but Khepri is laughing at Tupac's antics. Soon, Dev joins him and they taunt Ra's dogs by belting out the chorus in uneven harmony. *It would be really handy to be human again,* is the last thing I think as a swan before I feel my body contort and turn me into just that.

I blink in surprise to find myself standing on the rooftop, a woman once more, still clad in my prison wear—*that was easy.* I'll have to test if it works that quickly in reverse but, for now, I open my mouth, glad that the words 'and it burns, burns, burns' come out and not a lightning bolt. It's all fun and games until the jackals turn their heads towards Khepri, Raiden, and me.

"Oh, shit," I sputter.

"An excellent idea!" Khepri crows and Raiden and I look at him like he's nuts. But he just continues, "Raiden, use your lightning to force Anubis' bitches back while I create a pit of poo!"

I grimace at this idea, but Raiden quickly raises his arms and sends arcs of electricity shooting from the tips at the now howling group of female dogs. Behind the dogs but before the ring of fire that protects the other half of our group, Khepri is concentrating on a space on the ground. What was once asphalt roof top now seems to be a bubbling pool of mud—until I get a whiff of it. The crazy man actually created a *pit of poo*. I have no idea if it sinks into the apartment of the humans dwelling just below us or not. I hope not. I hope the supernatural magic at work is one of those invisible-to-human-eyes type of things. It seems like our battle was, because I didn't hear a ton of car crashes when my sisters littered the sky with their trashy attitudes.

Slowly, but methodically, Raiden drives the jackals back until they tumble into the gloppy puddle of crap.

Their barks of disgust make me wince in semi-pity. Futilely, they struggle to get out, but only seem to submerge themselves deeper. It's not until they are waist-high in shit that I realize they are *sinking*. Khepri didn't just make a pit of poo—*it's quickshit*, or quick-sand made of fecal matter, if you will.

I'm torn between horror, amusement, and a little awe. *Who would have thought that poop would be so useful?*

When the jackals take their last breath and descend into their crappy graves, I turn to Khepri, who is smirking evilly. He clearly takes a lot of joy in his strange powers.

"Khepri, you've got your shit together," I compliment.

He smiles and gives me a thumbs up. I give him one back, all while thinking, this man and my Uncle Loki should *never* meet. I shudder to think of what those two could come up with together. All kinds of stupid shit.

Raiden sees my shiver of fear. "Are you cold?" he asks. He puts a muscular arm around my shoulders and I'm pulled close to his delicious abs. My fingers run over them, totally by accident, not because I'm in any way pretending to be off balance for the excuse to touch them, or his happy trail.

My naughty thoughts are interrupted by Tupac clearing his throat and I attempt to make my face blank.

He drops the ring of fire and both Dev and Lover walk over to stand with the rest of us. My eyes travel from Raiden's black eyes, to Khepri's kohl-lined blue, then to Tupac's smug brown orbs, and finally to Dev's panicked hazel brown gaze. I'm so relieved that everyone is safe, I can feel my legs collapsing underneath me. Strong hands catch me before I can fall maladroitly on my ass, and I turn to find *Dad*.

Shocked is an understatement. I'm at a total loss. My relief morphs right back into panic. Did my stepmoms get home and lie to him? Did my sisters say I started this battle? Does he know I took the cart and broke into Ra's prison?

"What in Niflheim[1] is going on here?" he demands.

Tanny and Tangy bleat in the background as I trip over my words in my rush to explain everything to him.

I'm sure whatever I spew out is a jumbled mess that makes no sense, but Dad pulls me in for a fierce hug when I finish and I can feel him pouring all his support and love into it. I revel in this hug—*and my guilt.*

"Dad—I'm sorry ... about everything. For making you sick, for taking your goats and your hammer. But I swear that I've been taking great care of all three of them."

The mighty Thor gives me a sardonic smile and walks over to Tangy and Tanny to pet them. I join him and quietly hand him his prized weapon.

"I missed you, my favorite one," he croons.

"Aw! Thanks, Dad!"

"I was talking to Mjölnir. You're my youngest or Earthly off-spring."

"That's whack, Pops."

Thor puffs up his chest.

"Real parents don't have favorites. As it were, I'm leaving everything to the hammer and goats."

I roll my eyes—of course, the sentient tool and the Devil's caprine offspring will inherit it all when Dad crosses over.

Dad chuckles at my peeved look and gives me one of his own.

"Next time, daughter—*ask for my help*," he commands.

I feel my eyebrows raise.

"Dad … I illegally set out to free my best friend from jail. I don't think that's something you would have helped me with."

"Maybe not directly, but the clouds have ears, my dear, and they whisper the truths to me. I know what's going on more than you think I do, and you need to know that I'm here for you. I will find your stepmoms and sisters, take them back to Asgard with me and deal with them."

His mouth sets in a grim line at this announcement before softening again.

"Keep the girls and Mjölnir for now. Only someone very powerful could wield him."

"Him?! Ha, I knew that hammer had a dic—I mean, I knew he was a boy," I hastily correct, making all the guys behind me groan.

So far, they have been silent, letting my father and I have our moment, but Dev surprises me by stepping up and addressing Dad. I'm not sure if it's temerity or if he doesn't understand exactly who he's addressing.

My stomach falls.

This entire exchange with Dad has gone a million times better than I ever dreamed it would, but I have a feeling that it's about to take a nosedive.

"Sir. Ah, hi. I'm Dev, Val's boyfriend—I mean friend … I mean friend who's a boy…" he trails off awkwardly, staring at me in panic as his ears turn fire-engine red.

I gulp. Is he seriously looking for me to define our brand-new relationship in front of my father?
Right now?

Lover sniggers under his breath.

Raiden chimes in, "We're concubines." He tosses an arm over Khepri's shoulder. "Right old buddy? We're all Val's—"

I step in front of all the guys to block Dad's view. "Sorry. I had to hit him on the head with Mjoli and now he's a little …" I do the crazy circle on the side of my head.

Dev tries to break up this parade of awkward moments he started.

"What I meant to say, sir, is that I'm sorry I took your sacred goats and thanks for understanding Val. She's … pretty amazing."

Even though Dad still is giving poor Dev a stern look, there's a marked twinkle in his eyes.

"That she is—the first swan Valkyrie in over five thousand years!" Dad smoothly ignores Raiden, who's arguing in whispers with Khepri. Some nonsense about going next.

I blush. In my panic at seeing Dad, I'd forgotten that I had finally come into my powers.

Dad bumps my shoulder. "Took you long enough, Sigrdrifa," he teases and I roll my eyes.

"Like I had any say in it," I counter.

"Actually," my Dad says gently, "you did. I've always sensed your powers lurking under the surface—they just needed the right nudge to be unleashed. I thought that at some point, the bullying and cattiness from your sisters—and yes, even my wives—would force them to the forefront. After a time, I realized you weren't like them, however. You fought back—but always with your words and your humanity." He runs a hand through his dark red hair and sighs. "Being a parent is quite difficult sometimes. I knew I could force your gifts to appear, but the very thing that everyone else despised you for, you loved. Your humanity. How could I take that from you and force you to be like us? So, I let you just be you. I love you no matter what, but please know that I maybe hold you in a slightly higher regard than the rest of your siblings."

"But not more than Tangy and Tanny?" I joke.

"Daughter, they're magical goats—stop trying to compete with them because you will never win."

I laugh and stick my tongue out at him.

"Now, I have quite the mess to clean up but, first, a little parting gift. Everyone, get into the cart."

No one waits to do as Thor commands. Every single one of the guys scrambles to be first into the back of the cart. I giggle a little at how quick they are to accommodate him.

I ride up front next to dad as he takes the reins. "So, concubines …" he whispers.

"Nope. Nuh-uh. 'It's time for Animaniacs …'" I start to sing to stave off a conversation that I never ever want to have.

We fly a short distance away before landing in a small clearing in a forest about half an hour from the city. It's actually quite close to the farm where I grew up with mom. Dad gets out and takes a deep breath.

He traces a hand over a meadow flower and stares at the trees.

"I love Asgard—but I also love the human world. I met your mom here. She was picking wild flowers," he comments to me and I store the information away like a golden treasure.

The bright yellow wildflowers take on a whole new layer of beauty for me. Suddenly, Dad starts laughing uproariously.

"Um, what's so funny?" I wonder.

"I was just remembering the time that I met your grandpa … I might have let some thunder accidentally rip, if you know what I mean," he chuckles unabashedly. "Your mom went on to introduce me as the God of Flatulence. She was such a little smartass— exactly where you got it from—but it's what I loved about her most. Her warmth, humor, and *normalcy.* Your mom gave me something no other being ever has."

I smile, loving this moment. Dad doesn't talk very much about her because I know it hurts him to bring her up. I wait to see if he'll say anything else but, instead, he just claps. And out of freaking nowhere—*a house falls from the sky to the ground.*

"Holy shit!" I cry. "Good thing I'm not the Wicked Witch of the East or I would be one dead witch."

Dev and Tupac laugh. Everyone else just gives me a blank look.

"Nevermind," I say. "Dad, where the heck did this come from?"

I stare in wonder at the tiny house—*and I do mean tiny.* It's like those single room kid's playhouses that apparently are now all the rage to live in. I should know—I sold enough of them at the Home Depot.

The house is brown planks with dark green shutters with tiny empty planter boxes under each window, and a red front door.

"Er ...wow. Gee, thanks, Dad. That was super nice of you," I'm half-lying, half-sincere.

It *was* super nice of him ... except, I can barely fit into his 'house'. Dad gives me a quick peck on the forehead. He tosses a head nod to the guys and gives a disgusting number of cooing kisses to Tangy and Tanny before striding off again in the direction we came from—probably to collect the rest of his asshole family.

I grimace. I felt sorrier for him than I did me. Poor guy has to take them back to his house and deal with them—me? I'll just turn into a swan and fry their asses if they come near me again.

"OK, everyone. You heard Dad … into the house!"

Dev looks at me helplessly and I shrug in response before I march over and swing open the front door. I manage to squeeze my lanky body through the miniature frame and I fall into *an expansive foyer*. Holy shit-nuggets—this house is like the Weasley's tent!

"I love magic," I quote Harry reverently as I stare inside the space that has now easily quadrupled in size. It looks like the foyer of some expensive ski lodge, still wood, but with eighty foot ceilings and the entire hull of a viking ship hung overhead and infused with twinkling lights like it's some crazy chandelier. "Guys! Get in here! Quick—oh, and bring the goats, too!"

"Val, there's no way goats will—what are you guys doing?" I hear Dev question my instructions. But I also hear the stomp of hooves.

One by one, the guys crouch to come in, wide smiles stretching their faces as they see the interior.

They don't call my Dad 'mighty' for nothing, but *damn*, he outdid himself this time. It's hysterical to see Dev try and shove Tanny through the door while she tries to bite his nose off. I grab her by the collar, careful to twist my hand *away* from her mouth. Tangy follows and then Dev, who stares in open-mouthed wonder.

"Wow," he exhales. "This is fucking badass."

I wander up the stairs set back on the left side of the giant entryway and go down a hallway with a row of five doors—*bedrooms*. I grin when I see the first one decked out in Egyptian relics.

"Oh, Khepri! Dad made you a room!" I call.

The Egyptian god races up the stairs. He pauses for a second when he sees what's inside before he bounds into the room, hooting with joy.

"It's just like my old temple before Ra the Cunt-Faced Fucker destroyed it!" he yells in obvious delight and my heart constricts to hear his unabashed joy. He never says so, but I know from Ve^2, my great uncle, that being a minor and mostly forgotten god can cut deeply.

I open the next door. There are red columns, stone lanterns, and a wooden shrine. The feeling that emanates from the room is pure peace. I turn back to the guys."Raiden, yours is next."

Raiden comes up with Lover and Dev trailing behind him. He steps into his room. At first, I'm a little worried that he might destroy something in his addled state. But he turns to me with reverence.

"Your father made my room like my family temple. It was my favorite place to go when I was a child and I would pray to my ancestors to bring them honor."

"Awww!" I coo. "That's so sweet, Mulan! I'll leave you to it, then."

Raiden looks confused when I call him the name of Disney's most badass heroine, but I move along and open the next door.

A burst of light filters through, nearly blinding me. "Lover! You're up!"

Tupac chuckles and mutters, "I'm always up around you," as he walks in—*and falls to his knees*. Oh shit! Is he having a heart attack? Can demigods have those? I've seen Asteio pass out drunk before so I know that some human frailties can be passed down to us. Quickly, Dev and I rush over.

"Are you okay?" I demand in worry.

"I'm … fine. More than fine."

He looks up at me and I swear that I see the sheen of tears in his eyes.

"This is exactly what my homeland looks like—it's been four hundred years, seventy six days, ten hours, and fourteen minutes since I've seen it."

Understanding now, I lean down and wrap him in a hug. He pulls me in tight against him and I can feel his joy. It's a warm, radiant thing, just like the sun. It soaks into my skin.

"I know it's not exactly the same—but welcome home," I whisper in his ear.

Lover barely turns his head, but it's enough to bring his mouth dangerously close to mine. The familiar electric charge that I feel in close proximity to any of the guys begins to hum between us. I hear Dev's gasp and Tupac and I spring apart. Carefully, I clear my voice.

"Alrighty. I'll just leave you to it, then. I guess." Wow, I'm awkward. "Later, Lover."

I practically run from the room with Dev hot on my heels. I know he wants to talk about what happened—but I don't—so, I quickly open his door to his room and shove him in. I expect a protest, but silence greets me. I peek inside to see what could have rendered my friend speechless and see computer screens filling the space from floor to ceiling along all four walls.

"Oh, wow," I say in shock.

I didn't even know Dad knew much about human technology.

"I love your dad," Dev murmurs and I burst into laughter.

"I'll be back," I tell him.

I walk out and open the fifth door—but it's a *bath-room*. Grumbling because I think Dad thought of everyone but me, I meander through the house. I go back downstairs. There's an impressive living room and a fully equipped and stocked kitchen, but still no extra bedroom. It's not until I come to a warded door on the complete opposite side of the house that I know I've finally found it. The instant my hand touches the handle, the door springs open to reveal my room from Dad's house, complete with Animaniac figurines and pictures of my mom and Dot.

"I love you, Dad," I tell the room, walking to my closet full of all my favorites.

I quickly change so that the guys and I can reconvene, but not before I collapse on my bed in a fit of giggles. Dad made my room warded and on the other side of the house not to protect me from outside threats—*but to keep me separated from the others*!

I laugh some more until my sides hurt and I let out an embarrassing honk—whoops! I'll have to watch out for that.

Poor Dad.

He had probably been hoping to keep at least one of his Valkyries pure—and thank Alfheim[3] that he can't read minds because my thoughts recently have been very *impure*. Raiden's statement from earlier fills my mind as I get ready for bed. I fall asleep to dreams of four naughty concubines.

16

TUPAC

"WE NEED A WAY TO ATTACK RA," KHEPRI SAYS, SHAKING his head as we stand around the kitchen in Thor's Habitat for Demi-Humanity house. It's become our unofficial hideout since Thor promised we were safe —*inside, at least*. I'm a little skeptical, however, because Val's stepmoms or sisters could possibly know about this place. And after that embarrassing defeat they just suffered, I'm pretty sure they're going to spread the word like a mockingbird. (I'm totally the better rapper.)

"No shit, Sherlock," I tell him as I pull out a kitchen stool and sit. I'm not exactly sure what Sherlock is, but I've seen that said online, so I know it's some kind of insult. Doubled with the 'no shit' to a shit god, I'm feeling pretty clever, you know?

"But if we attack Ra ... won't the sun fall from the sky?" Devin bites his lip and glances over at Val. They share this angsty glance.

I've never been jealous of someone else's angst before—but I am now—I want to play the angst game with that woman.

Any game really. My eyes drift to her nipples for a second, which I recall are the perfect coral pink, before I listen to the conversation.

"If another sun god doesn't pick it up, yeah, the sun will fall and destroy the earth," Khepri sighs.

Raiden shakes his head. "But, that would be the end of everyone. No earth and no humans means no gods," he says in a brief moment of lucidity, which disappears when he adds, "But, it would also mean the end of lima beans."

I scrunch my nose. "Yeah, let's not go the way of the dino gods."

Dev raises a finger in the air, pausing mid-sip. "Wait. Timeout. Dinos had gods?"

"They were way more intelligent than they were given credit for," I tell him, using my serious eyes. "There are abandoned worship sites for dinos all over the place."

Dev looks over at Val for confirmation. He doesn't quite believe me. Not as dumb as he looks.

When she rolls her eyes he flips me off, but Raiden surprises me by taking my side.

"The Japanese worship Godzilla, which is pretty much a dinosaur with the name god built right in. We have temples for him everywhere."

He beams a brilliant grin my way and I laugh at

both his stupidity and since before his "accident," I swear that he never smiled a day in his life. That god never had a happy day, and I bet when he jizzed he still frowned.

This concussion might be the greatest thing that's ever happened to him.

Khepri chimes in, "If we're done talking about fairy tales, and can continue with the Ra issue … we have a lot of problems with attacking him midday. Unfortunately, most of the other solar deities are less powerful than him."

"Even Apollo?" I ask. Those Greek assholes always get all the glory. Dev, who's now passing out coffee, hands me a steaming cup that may or may not have a loogie floating in it. I lick my lips and grin at him naughtily before I take a sip. If he thinks I have any sort of issues exchanging bodily fluids, he's got another thing coming. (Although, I meant that in a sexy way— swapping spit and loads and shit—not snot.)

Khepri's face grows red when he hears my question and he clears his throat uncomfortably, staring down at his own mug, which says Jewels Cafe and has a little ruby on it. "I don't know about Apollo. He and I … haven't gotten along for nearly a millennium."

I roll my eyes. "What happened, you bang that tree nymph of his?"

"No!" Khepri protests. "I just happened to think Pan was the better musician … and I ended up with donkey ears for a century because of it."[1]

I swallow a laugh, picturing the head guard with donkey ears. Damn, if we'd had the low down on that in the Back Hole, we would have made so many ass jokes to go along with the shit ones.

Next to me, Devin squints at him. "But, wasn't that a long time ago?"

"Gods don't forget," Val sighs, running a hand through her long, luscious hair.

Just watching her makes my heart pump faster. My eyes trace the line of her elegant neck and a bit of desperation seeps into my pores. She's let me touch her, let me watch her, will she ever let me …

My mouth is moving before I realize what I'm saying. "I could catch it."

All eyes turn to look skeptically at me.

"You?" Khepri scoffs, the arrogant asshole. "You aren't even a full god."

I narrow my eyes and grit my teeth. The urge to nut punch him is pretty damn strong, but he's got a hot cup of coffee near Val, so I resist.

Val sets her coffee down on the countertop and says, "I think that's a great idea."

My dick and the rest of my body twitches in excitement. The near-certain-death I'm probably facing fades to a distant worry-about-it-tomorrow kind of problem as Val's attention takes the forefront for today.

I smile down at her and she returns my look, which feels like the softest sunlight at the end of the afternoon.

Val steps over and grabs my hand. And suddenly, I can't judge Dev anymore for how smitten he looked after a little hand holding yesterday. Because I'm wearing the exact same expression on my face. There's something about Val. This electricity. And I'm not just talking about the lightning bolt she swallowed.

"I used to train with my dad," she tells me. "I might be able to help."

Khepri hurries to add his two cents. He stops right next to Val and peers down at her. "I should help, too. I'm better equipped to train him."

Raiden decides to chime in, too.

"I can make rain," he claims proudly.

"That's ... awesome. And training is all well and good if we end up having a plan to attack against Ra, but we don't have an idea of how we're going to protect ourselves *at all*," I point out.

Val presses her lips together. "That's true."

She turns to Khepri, "Why don't you help Tupac, while the three of us stay here and work on a plan—"

I interrupt. "I'd rather work with you," I tell Val quickly.

"That's ridiculous. I'm far more qualified—" Khepri starts to argue.

"You're a god!" I tell him. "That makes you completely unqualified to understand any of the issues a demigod might have. Plus, you were my captor for oh, I dunno, four centuries, and I had to listen when you told me to piss, so no—I'm done taking orders from you. Talk to the hand!" My rant gets a little more heated than I intended, but I realize even as the words fly out of my mouth that I mean them. I don't want to listen to an arrogant god spouting off shit like 'this is so easy' when it's not.

Val reaches out and squeezes my hand. She gives me an understanding smile. "Okay. I'm happy to practice with you."

Oh, how I wish practice was a metaphor for something else. There are so many things I want to "practice" on Val but the only one I get to do is the hand-holding as we leave the forest and walk until we have enough signal to call a rideshare car to take us to a local gym. Turns out, Thor's shack-turned-mansion-magic-house is near where Val grew up with her mom and sister and is about twenty minutes from the city. So, Val says she knows the perfect place for us to train.

When we walk in, I'm nearly blinded by the bright pink and purple paint. Every inch of the space is covered in mats that sink beneath your feet. And there's a sparkly unicorn on the far wall underneath the clock that would offend any true unicorn.[2]

"Where are we?" I wonder with a grimace.

"This place teaches kids' gymnastics, but it's mostly just girls who join," she tells me. "I went here for a little while when I was younger. My sister did gymnastics, so obviously, I had to try it. But I had to quit when … I went to live with my dad."

She is sharing her past with me. Among gods (and

demigods) information is a weapon. Information lets others see your vulnerabilities—lets them know how to attack you. I know less about previous cellmates that I spent centuries with than I now do about this beautiful brunette at my side.

The sadness in her voice tugs at me. I give her hand a squeeze and I trace a tender finger down her face.

But the owner of the building, a middle-aged human woman who's incredibly fit, comes out of an office to meet us, and totally ruins the moment. She shakes hands with Val as they talk about renting the place for a few hours.

While they chit-chat, I roam and touch some bars covered in chalk, then stride over to a strange bench that seems too small for giants but too large for humans.

Val rejoins me with a smile as the owner disappears out the front door to give us a bit of privacy. "So, I hope you're fast."

"Only when I have to be," I trace my hand up her arm, letting my innuendo settle over her.

She rolls her eyes. "Well, you have to be for this."

"Okay. But I want to be slow later. Super slow. Glacier slow."

Val shakes her head but there's a smile on her face. "I'm gonna start calling you One Track if you can't focus on anything else."

"Lover is a far better name," I tease.

She just sighs and goes to pull out some large foam

mats. I help. We set up an obstacle course around the room. Then she turns to me. "Your goal is to run the obstacle course with as big a ball of fire as you can, tossing it up and down. But, forewarning, if you burn this building down, you're gonna have to pay for it, and little five-year-olds in pigtails will sob until it's rebuilt."

My throat gets a little dry at that. But before I can respond, Val shifts into her swan. Her mouth opens and orange lightning zaps my ass.

I run, yelling at the low trick. She's playing dirty. She'll pay for that later. I form a ball of fire and try to toss and catch it as I dodge Val and leap over piled mats.

The first time, I trip and drop the fireball, I forget to put it out. I fall right through it, unharmed, incredibly glad I paid Stata Major[3] to fireproof my hair and clothes centuries ago, because though my body is technically fireproof, the hair (for some ungodly reason) isn't. And it's my best fucking feature. Women go gaga for it.

The smell of burnt plastic wafts over me—I'm going to be paying for that—and Val's swan beak nips my ass, making me jump.

"Hey! Ass play only in human form!" I scold her.

I've tried it other ways and the human way is literally the only pleasurable one.

The thought of Val playing with my ass spurs me to get up and get moving. The sooner we can figure out this sun-ball thing, the sooner she can try that biting thing again with her human teeth.

I magic up a fireball twice the size of the one I just dropped. It's roughly the size of one of the compact cars we rode over in. I toss it in the air, trying not to hit the ceiling. I keep my eyes on it as I run and jump over some more stacked mats.

But right as I grab it, Val shocks me in the ass.

Fuck!

I drop the fireball and know immediately that it's too big.

This place is gonna go up in flames. Fuck. I try to put it out by stomping then rolling on it. But I'm a sun god, not a water god. We should have brought Raiden The Concussed along.

I grab Val's hand and we book it toward the door. I hear a *whoosh* behind us as the flames climb the walls. We duck outside.

I turn to look back at the blaze. Since Incans never minted money, and I've basically just been released from jail I hope they'll take payment in the form of beautiful sunshiny days.

"Shit!" Val looks distressed. "It's a goner."

"Don't think shit's gonna help with that," Khepri's arrogant voice behind me says.

We turn to see the other three guys staring at us. All three of them have glazed looks and massive boners.

How did they even get here? Why isn't Raiden putting the fire out? But he doesn't even lift his fingers.

"What are you doing—" my question trails off when I see what's behind all three guys. Or, I guess I shouldn't say what. I should say who.

Guess practice is over. Ready or not, the fight just came to us.

17

VAL

"Fuck sticks," I curse as I see the golden-haired woman floating on half a clamshell in midair behind my guys.

Aphrodite glares at me in a way that makes my pussy shrivel and grow dry.

Her hand is extended in midair, her fingers curled like she's grasping something, but nothing is there. She jerks her hand forward and all three of my guys lurch forward, groaning as their hands reach for their rock-solid cocks.

She's leading them around by their dicks. Literally.

Fury fills me along with a strong sense of possessiveness. Those dicks belong to me.

Aphrodite ignores the three car pileup that happens because she's blocking the road. But I can't.

The furious goddess is attacking us in human territory.

I turn to Raiden, whose unfocused gaze is far more normal and less heartbreaking it's been for the past several days. "Can you blow us out of here?"

"No blowing!" Aphrodite screeches.

But, Raiden's been working on a glass-half-full for awhile now and he quickly whips up a tornado that sweeps us out of the city and into a cornfield. The stalks are nearly to our shoulders, and the bright scent of fresh dirt fills my nose as the tornado dissipates, leaving us standing in a crop circle of decimated stalks when we land.

Aphrodite's screech of fury as she nearly falls out of her shell reminds me of a cat in a catfight.

I have a feeling that's exactly what this is going to be. The love goddess hates being humiliated.

As Aphrodite struggles to her feet, Dev turns to me. He looks like a guy about to come, jaw sagging, face blank and brain switched off, but underneath that flat gaze, he manages to mutter the words, "I'm sorry. This is my fault."

His fault? How can he possibly blame himself when I'm the one who asked for his help?

I don't have time to protest, because seconds later, Aphrodite straightens. "I'm going to make you rue the day—"

Tupac holds up a hand, like this is school. "I'm sorry. Aren't you the Greek love goddess? I'm from another continent and all, sister, but aren't you supposed to be all 'make love not war?'"

Aphrodite's growl of fury is interrupted by a honk overhead as a pair of swans fly by. Khepri lifts a hand and suddenly two streaks of swan shit plop onto Aphrodite's face.

I take a step backward. "Crap. That was a mistake."

"No it wasn't," says Khepri, his face still dull but his voice furious. "It was a shitty decision."

"I thought it was pooptacular," Tupac quips.

Aphrodite growls as she lifts her dress to wipe her cheeks. She changes her hand position and that releases my guys from their hard-ons. They all sigh, in relief or disappointment I'm not sure, as their dicks deflate.

But that's the only relief they get before Aphrodite is screaming across the field, "I curse all four of you to be attracted to gods damned swans!"

Her curse is met with silence.

Until Raiden giggles. Khepri smacks him in the chest, and mutters, "Shhh."

But the goddess can clearly see her curse doesn't have its intended effect. With an unattractive snort of fury, she bends and grabs something inside her clamshell.

She holds up a gleaming golden triangular thingie— I have no idea what it actually is—and says, "By the power of Ra, I command you! Come attack them!"

Seconds later, the sky fills with shadows. And it's not full of birds or planes ... or superheros. It's full of falling mummies.

The sound when they hit the ground and their
bones crack makes me wince. The fact that they pull
themselves up to their spindly feet afterward? That
terrifies me.

All around me, the guys take up fighting stances.
Devin runs to the edge of the crop circle, grabs a cornstalk, and tries to break it, but after several frantic
pulls, he can't.

"A little help?" he asks Tupac, who tosses his mullet
behind his shoulders and then burns a clean line across
the base of several stalks.

Dev grabs one and wields it like a spear with a furry
end. It reminds me a little bit of one of those feather
tipped toys people make for cats.

Only, these mummies aren't cats. With glowing red
eyes, and horrific moans, this feels like a moment out
of a cheesy scary movie.

When the first mummy touches my arm and I feel
its bony hand encircle my wrist, I quickly upgrade
from cheesy scary movie to full-on horror film.

I stare at the mummy's rotten nose for a second
before self preservation instincts kick in and I transform into my swan.

The mummy's hands slide off me and I take to
the air.

"Are you fucking kidding me?" Aphrodite screams.
"You had no powers four days ago. I change my
curse—"

I cuff her with my wing before she can finish her

sentence.

She ducks and starts crying. "No birds in my hair! No birds in my hair!"

I'm not sure what that's about but I'll take it, because my guys and I have enough to worry about with the mummies she has conjured up. There have to be at least fifty of them.

Tupac has torched a couple, and is using a fire shield over his arm, like the shield of some great medieval knight, to hold them off.

Dev's bonking them ineffectively with his corny spear.

Khepri's pulled his shitsand trick again and is trying to coax several into it, but they seem to trace his footsteps rather than go directly at him, which is making his technique rather ineffective.

Raiden is … I think he's trying to conjure up a storm. But the mummies that he shoots water at just swell like water balloons before latent molds and bacteria bloom between their bandages like pustules.

One of the swollen fuckers turns to go for Dev and he smacks it with his corn stalk. It pops. The mummy collapses but the smell it releases leaks out over the field.

Tupac immediately turns and shoots a jet of fire at it, which just adds the smell of smolder to the mix.

"Don't touch the wet ones!" Khepri orders, stepping up and taking charge. "Tupac, burn them up! Raiden, I need another windstorm!"

Aphrodite struggles upright and I immediately open my beak. Orange lightning sizzles through her and her body jolts around as her hair stands on end. I pull back my power before it can make her bald, because I think if I do that, the feud between us will never end.

Instead, I flap my wings so I can get a bit higher and I focus on her minions. Raiden is struggling to make a second windstorm, possibly because a mummy has tackled him to the ground.

I honk, and I shoot creamsicle-colored lighting at the mummy, grateful that Raiden won't be hurt by it.

The mummy immediately stops attacking and stands. It raises its arms so that they are shoulder height, wrists dangling limply. It looks … like Franken-stien's monster.

Holy crapola! Did my lighting somehow reprogram it? I open my beak and send out another wave of light-ning, hitting at least five more mummies, who all assume the same position.

I fly over to Tupac and land behind his fire shield.

"You look so damn PHAT!" Tupac declares. "Pretty hot and tempting, get those feathers over here." I trans-form into my human body, ignoring him.

I turn to the mummies and yell, "Go grab Aphrodite!"

The six mummies that I zapped immediately turn in the opposite direction and stomp toward the goddess of love.

Meanwhile, Dev flips his cornstalk around like a baseball bat and decapitates a mummy, whose head pops off and slowly unravels down his front until a skull lands at the figure's feet. The headless body tumbles sideways into Khepri's quickshit and slowly sinks.

Raiden finally gets his tornado going and it sucks in at least thirty mummies straight off, but with the quickshit nearby, it makes the entire field smell like a giant fart. I gag and cover my nose with one hand, waving the other in an attempt to get Raiden to hurry.

Unfortunately, he misreads my signal as a direction to make the dustdevil go left, directly through the quickshit. The windfunnel quickly sucks up the liquid feces and turns into a literal shit storm.

I point straight at Aphrodite and Raiden turns the F-1 in direction. Actually, now that I think about it, it should be called an F-U.

The love goddess is fighting off some of the mummies I sent after her, but when she sees the brown whirling mass, she forgets about the mummy whose skeletal hand is stuck on her boob. She grabs the edges of her shell and tries to make it fly backward.

She's too late. The pull of the tornado is already drawing her in. The mummy attached to her breast is wrenched away into the wind. Aphrodite ducks low and clings to her shell.

"Oh no you don't!" Tupac calls and shoots a flame at her ass that makes her yelp and lose her grip.

And that's how the goddess of love becomes a shitshow.

As soon as she is sucked into the storm, Tupac flames the remaining mummies on the ground.

I just watch the chaos as Raiden slowly moves the tornado across the field away from us.

Dev comes over to stand beside me. "Thought she was hot shit, didn't she?"

Tupac walks over and gives him a high five. "Pretty sure she's got shit for brains, though."

"We kicked the shit out of her," Khepri waltzes over, a huge grin on his face. "I'm loving these crappy jokes."

Raiden drops the tornado at the far side of the field, letting Aphrodite and the jumble of shitstained bones fall in a heap. The goddess of love disappears in a bright flash of light as Raiden joins us and squints, biting his lip, his face contorted in what looks like pain. I rush forward and grab his bicep, sliding my hand down his arm. "Are you hurt?" I look him over.

He shakes his head and stutters. "Now, Aphro... Aphro... she's shitfaced."

I laugh and sweep the hot-as-sin god into a hug as the puns continue all around me. I laugh until my ribs hurt and Raiden sweeps me into his arms because I can't stand anymore.

I laugh until I see a fascinating, hesitant look in his eyes. Then I pause, breathless, as he leans forward and places the tiniest kiss on the corner of my lips.

18

RAIDEN

"We make a great team," I compliment my best friend once we are safely back in the house. Dev and Tupac wander off ahead of us, muttering things like 'showers' and 'brush my teeth 'til my tongue falls off' as they climb the stairs.

Khepri gives me a funny look before softly smiling.

"Yeah, I guess we kind of do," he agrees, scratching at his chin.

"And don't get me started on you," I say to Val, who is currently becoming the center of my universe.

She's dressed in tight athletic clothes that show off every curve. And it doesn't matter that bits are ripped or singed or smelly, because underneath all of that are luscious curves and a kami[1] that's more beautiful than any I've ever seen.

"That bad?" she jokes.

"That amazing," I correct. "I ... worship you," I announce fervently, falling to my knees in front of her.

She appears startled at my admission, but Khepri gives me a frown.

"Oh, no you don't!" he commands, dragging me to my feet.

"What?" I ask in confusion.

"Uh-oh, Bi-Polar is jealous," Val laughs tauntingly.

"Bi-Polar?" I wonder.

"It's my nickname for him. You have one, too."

"I do? What is it?!" I blurt out in delight.

This vision gave me a nickname?

Thunder rumbles in my chest, like the start of a beautiful rainstorm.

"Kung-Fu."

"I like that much better than Mulan," I confirm and Val chuckles.

"You're really a fun guy, Raiden," she observes, placing a small pale hand to my chest.

My body tightens at the sight of her touching me and I groan. She's like a banquet—a delectable feast—and I'm *starving*.

Val's eyes meet mine and I swear I see the same hunger reflected there. Without thinking, I lean down and capture her lips with mine—they are as petal-soft as I imagined.

I groan even louder and I hear Khepri growl.

I quickly break my impromptu kiss and step back from Val, feeling guilty for some reason that I can't explain. Until I can. I realize where my guilt stems as I stare into Khepri's blue eyes.

"I'm sorry," I apologize to Val. "I didn't mean to do that."

"You didn't want to kiss me?" Val queries. She looks a little disappointed.

I rush to grab her hand and stroke it. "No, I did—I do, but Khepri doesn't like it ... I think he likes you, too. Actually," I whisper conspiratorially, "I think we *all* like you."

I shoot Khepri a nervous glance to find him glowering at me. Yep—he definitely likes her, too, and clearly doesn't want me kissing her. But how come Dev can kiss her? Why isn't Khepri mad at him? Is it because he and I are best friends? I pout a little at how unfair it is, but Val soothes me.

"I like all you guys, too," she confesses and my heart soars.

As does my dick.

I give her a clumsy hug, trying not to rub my erection against her long legs, but fail miserably. It's just they are so smooth and perfect and those thighs. I pull back.

The look on her face is one torn between amusement and arousal.

"Sorry," I apologize again. "I'll think of something else ... lima beans ... rodents ... forest fires ... sex—*no*! Not sex. Ahhhh!"

Now, Val *and* Khepri are covering their mouths,

laughing at me and I hang my head in shame.

I'm nothing but a joke to them. I walk off feeling like a raincloud is looming over my head. I look up to see there actually is one! My sadness must have created it. I go into my room and shut the door, trying to make the cloud go away—*it starts raining on me, instead.*

I hear a soft knock on the door and Val pokes her head in when I don't answer.

"Kung-Fu? Are you ok? We're sorry," she says and I see Khepri standing behind her.

He doesn't seem as repentant as Val, but her words help make the rain slowly ebb away.

"Can we come in?" she asks.

"Are you going to laugh at me some more?"

"No. Raiden—don't be upset. It was just the jump from forest fires to sex. I just … the logic of that ..." She trails off, aware she is digging herself into a hole.

"Everything leads back to sex thoughts when I'm around you," Khepri says. "So, it's an easy mistake to make."

Val ignores his confession, focused on me. "Raiden, I need you to forgive me. I'm so sorry. Nearly every other thought I have around you is hot and bothered too. I mean, look at you," she gestures to my near-perfect physique, hewn by centuries of exercise and magic, "I promise you that I find you *very* attractive."

For some reason, a streak of vindictive triumph fills me at her words and I send Khepri a gloating look. His dark face instantly becomes shadowed with rage and I shake my head in confusion. *Why am I taunting my best friend? It is most dishonorable of me—and the one thing I definitely remember about myself is that honor is everything.*

Val sends Khepri an exasperated glare. "You know I find you equally good-looking, so stop your sulking," she orders to the surly Egyptian god. "I like you both *in equal measure.*"

"Then, we should have sex together, all three of us," I announce without really thinking of what I'm saying.

Both Val's and Khepri's face go blank.

Perhaps it is not honorable to propose this? I cross my arms over my chest in worry. I can't remember.

Val's mouth opens and closes a few times before she can get the words out, "Did ... did he just suggest we have a threesome?" She looks up at Khepri, who is subtly adjusting his hard dick as he nods.

"A threesome?" I inquire, rolling the unfamiliar word around my head.

"It's when three people have sex," Khepri clarifies dryly for me.

"Oh!" I exclaim in understanding.

Clearly, if there's a word for it, it is not dishonorable—I just didn't say it correctly! Cheer brightens my mood and my rain cloud, which had stopped leaking, completely disappears.

"Apologies, Val and Best Friend Ever, I meant, would you like a threesome to keep everything equal?"

I beam at them proud that I have come up with such a sound plan.

"I've never done anything like that," Val admits. Her cheeks turn a delicious red as she ducks her head and tucks a strand of brunette hair behind one ear.

"I don't think I have, either—have I, Khepri?" I ask with a raised brow as I step closer to Val.

"How in Duat should I know?!" he chokes out in a horrified voice.

"I just figured it's something that I would tell you."

Khepri scowls up at the ceiling of my temple room. "Dude—I don't think your dick has seen any action in years."

"I think you might be right," I concur. "It's always talking to me and I get that impression."

"His penis *talks* to him?" Val whispers to Khepri.

"All guys' cocks talk to them. That's why there's the saying about thinking with the wrong head," I clarify for Val. Clearly her education has been a bit lacking. "Mine is named Hanma." I gesture down at him. He strains to reach Val. He'd really love to shake hands with her.

"Hanma? Like rhymes with grandma?"

"Hanma like hammer, like pounding," I gently correct.

"Oh please," my best friend cannot contain his eye roll.

I ignore him because Val moves closer to me, staring down at Hanma.

"Right," she drawls, licking her lips. She sounds breathy when she asks, "So ... what does Hanma say?"

"That you're the most beautiful woman ever," I praise— it's the truth!

Val is perfect.

"Whelp, Kung-Fu's dick is hands-down my favorite." She reaches out and puts a perfect palm around Hanma.

Bliss.

"Wait a fucking minute!" Khepri snaps, stomping forward so he's directly behind Val and she's sand-wiched between us. "You haven't even heard what my dick has to say about you!"

"Honestly, you and Lover can keep your cock convos to yourselves. I'm a little afraid of the things they think and say to you."

Khepri growls and his hands go to her hips. "Woman," he warns.

"I'm going to light some candles," I interject before my best friend can spontaneously combust. I reluctantly step back from Val, but clearly, Khepri needs a moment with her.

"Should we leave you to pray, er, whatever you do in here?" Val offers.

"Oh, I'm not lighting them to pray—it's to set the mood for our threesome."

I walk away to do just that and Val whisper-wonders, "Is this really going to happen?"

Khepri pulls her backward against his iron-hard dick.

In answer, I take off my shirt and her eyes grow

extremely large. They are so pretty and remind me of storm clouds that are swollen with need, too full, just like my cock, building to that moment when they can rain.

"Is something wrong?" I ask in trepidation.

"N-n-n-o," she stammers. "You're just built like a god."

"Aren't I a god?" I query in bewilderment. Did I forget that, too?

"Yes, you're a god," she clarifies. "It's a human saying —it means you're very muscular."

"Which is good, right?" I demand.

Khepri ignores me and brings his lips to Val's neck as she stares at me.

"One hundred percent," she confirms breathily. "Muscles are one hundred percent sexy."

I feel a confident grin stretch my lips.

My intended mate finds me sexy.

"Bestie—show Val your muscles," I direct Khepri.

"No," he spits out curtly, before returning to her neck and running his teeth down the side.

"Why? Are you embarrassed—oh! You don't have any muscles," I realize. I just embarrassed my best friend in front of the woman he likes. "I'm sorry—"

"Oh, for pharaoh fuck's sake, I have muscles!" he declares, stepping back from Val and ripping his shirt off over his head.

Sure enough, his chest and abdomen resemble mine —but his skin is many shades darker than my bronzed flesh and he appears leaner than me. When I glance at Val, she seems to be in a stupor.

"What do you think?" I urge. Hanma is hungry for more compliments.

"You both are otherworldly," she decrees, and I preen a little under her praise. Hanma surges to life, pulsing with need. "But … I don't have relationships with gods."

"Wait—what? Why?" I cry. Horror and dismay roll through me, breaking up the sexual storm brewing between the three of us like nasty little rays of sunlight cut through cumulonimbus wonders. She's stopping this threesome before it even started!

"Gods are … dangerous. I don't want to get involved with them."

"But we're different," I almost pout.

"You are different," she agrees and my spirits soar again at her words.

"Then, let me kiss you again. But, first, kiss Khepri to make it fair."

"No—it's way more complicated than tha—" Val starts, but Khepri cuts her off with his mouth.

Val's back is to Khepri's chest and he has her head twisted to the side. I can see his tongue slide sensuously in and out of her mouth and I long to kiss her in the same way. I step up to her front and press my chest to hers. Both Khepri and I are touching her and something familiar sparks through my body and seems to race into hers. Instantly, she arcs into me and cries out passionately.

The strong scent of her arousal hits me and a memory drifts into my consciousness—Val asking if we can smell orgasms. I ignore it momentarily and pull her face to me to cover her lips with mine. With a moan, I kiss her just as Khepri did—with my tongue. Sensation after sensation pours into my body the longer Val and I kiss, and some part of me recognizes that she came when Khepri and I both touched her.

She came when we both touched her ...

The words keep running through my head, over and over and over, until a dam breaks free in my mind and the world spins around me. I wrench away from her and stare in horror.

"What in the sweet fuck is happening right now?!" I roar in anger, suddenly—and finally—coming back into my full faculties.

Val looks just as confused as I've felt until two seconds ago and Khepri wears his trademark sneer.

"Well, well, Raiden the Fuckstick is back and just in time for a threesome."

"WHAT?!" I scream, making Val flinch.

"Take a moment to think about everything that's happened," he counters.

For once, I actually do as the little pissant suggests. My mind zooms from one sickening memory to the next.

She was a prisoner.

We were guards.

She broke out.

Khepri … and I helped.

"You look like you're going to puke," Khepri points out gleefully.

"Yeah—well, I just might." It's the truth—I've basically spent the last however many days metaphorically sucking this prick's cock. My stomach churns. I fucking hate Khepri. Of all the gods in all the universes … I can't believe I called him best friend.

"Well, I'm glad you got your faculties back before you really embarrassed yourself," Kheprick continues.

"And just what the fuck is that supposed to mean?" I snap.

"That this 'threesome' would have been a joke on your part," he taunts.

"Bullshit!" I still want Val. Pissed as I am. Hanma and I still surge with energy at the sight of her, the smell of her. Nothing about being with her would be a joke.

"Oh, yeah? Prove it!" Khepri challenges.

I lunge forward and gather Val into my arms the same time that Khepri leaps for her. I get there first and pull her into me, kissing her passionately—angrily.

How dare they shame my name and my family with their farce—acting like we were all good friends. Belatedly, I remember the curse I feared was placed on me to make me hunger so for Val, but I just don't care anymore.

My hands roam down her sides and tweak her pebbled nipples and I shove my pelvis into hers. Hanma takes over, telling me, "She's a disease in our bloodstream—*I have to purge her from my body and this is the only way.*"

19

VAL

SHOCK TEARS THROUGH MY SYSTEM AS RAIDEN KISSES me. Gone is the playful man that I've come to adore over the last few days, in his place stands a furious god —*one who hates demis*. His hands roam my body and being sandwiched between Khepri and him is indescribable ...

And wrong.

"Stop," I command, trying to shove Raiden back a little.

His face is the familiar, wrathful thundercloud of ire that I saw before his ... accident with Dad's hammer. I wince a little—I can't entirely blame him for being pissed. Khepri refuses to give me any quarter and crowds my back even more, making me squirm.

"You want this, my khen[1]—I can *smell* it."

I flush in hot embarrassment, making even Kung Fu snicker around his pissy sneer. Thankfully, it bolsters

ANN DENTON & MJ MARSTENS

my courage to straighten my spine when my entire body wants to liquify into a puddle at their feet.

"Firstly, why are you calling me Ken? Secondly, yes, I can admit to wanting you both—*physically*. You two are very … um …"

"Khen is the ancient Egyptian word for swan. And perhaps you are searching for the word *virile*?" Khepri supplies.

"Chauvinistic?" Raiden offers helpfully and I glare.

"I liked you better when you were dumb," I snap. "No woman likes a man who's chauvinistic! Ugh! Listen, I don't do gods. End of story."

"You did Tupac," Khepri points out in a wounded voice.

"He's a demi," Raiden counters condescendingly.

"First off, I didn't do him … yet," I hedge, because even though my former cellmate often borders on ridiculous, he also has this genuinely gentlemanly quality that I love. "But, the very thing you look down upon him—*and me*—for, is the same reason I'm drawn to him. His humanity cancels his snobbish, I'm-better-than-you, dick god side!"

Raiden blinks at my tirade, seemingly taken aback at the depth of my emotions about full gods—but he doesn't get it. I can feel the tears sting my eyes thinking of everything that's happened in my life simply because I'm only *half*-goddess.

"Hey," Khepri says softly, turning me to him. His brow furrows and his kohl-lined eyes soften as he traces my cheek. "Look at me. I don't look down on you because of your lineage—I think you're amazing, just like the Demigodling. I can't speak for Raidong over here—"

"Fuck off, Kheprick, you traitorous bastard!"

"Ok, woah! Everyone calm down. What are you two —five? *Raidong? Kheprick?*"

Khepri snickers. "Admit they're funny," he chuckles.

"They're childish," I correct.

"They're supposed to be," Khepri sighs. "Are you going to tell us why you hate full gods so much? Aside from the obvious."

"What's the obvious?" I wonder.

"That your family—minus your father—are a bunch of fuckwits," Raiden attests, taking me by surprise.

"Fuckwits … that's a good word for my sisters and stepmoms. I'll have to use that one if I'm unfortunate enough to ever have a family dinner again. And, I really don't want to talk about this. It's personal," I state primly.

Both guys roll their eyes and I almost laugh at how similar they are—I bet they would *love* to hear that.

"Let me guess," Raiden snorts derisively, making me long to throat punch him, "You dated a full god and he was a fuckwit, too. And, *now*, you lump all of us gods together for one asshole's mistakes?"

"Kind of like how you lump all demis together because of what one god—Ra the Shit Wizard—thinks and says!" I snap back hotly.

"Hey!" Khepri yells, "I'm the only shit wizard around here!"

I try to maintain my stern glare, but end up laughing. *Dammit Khepri!* It's impossible to stay angry after a good shit pun.

We're quiet for a moment and Raiden stares at his hands.

"You're right," he finally whispers, surprising both Khepri and me with his confession. "I've only ever thought of the gods, of our honor, of what my parents said and their allegiance with Ra—but ... these past few days have accorded me an unhindered point of view from the demis and I realize that I never took responsibility for forming my own unbiased opinion. I ... was a sheep," he admits, ashamed.

Seeing how sad he looks makes my chest pulse, but not with anger anymore, with sad recognition. I walk over and wrap my arms around his waist, hugging him tightly.

"Then, we've been sheep together because I've done exactly the same thing, and as you said—I lumped all full-gods in with my bad experience from just one, but I know deep down that's wrong, unfair, and—most importantly—untrue."

"Now that that's settled, we can get this threesome underway!" Khepri jokes, smacking his hands and rubbing them together.

"Only if Val agrees," Raiden counters. His eyes hold mine for a long minute.

"You still want to?" I ask him, feeling a bit insecure until a smile stretches across Raiden's face and his eyes scan my body, blatantly checking me out in a way that sends a delicious thrill up my spine.

"Val, put the man out of his misery and touch his dick. I don't know if he's even been with a woman!" Khepri stage-whispers, earning a dark glower from Raiden.

"I could say the same for you!" Kung-Fu shoots back.

"Ugh!" I cry, throwing my hands up in the air. "Am I going to have to touch both your dicks to shut you two up?!"

"Whatever you need to tell yourself, sweetheart. Here, let me help you," Khepri purrs, pulling down the front of his pants.

Instantly, his very hard *and* very large cock springs forth. His hand can't even cover half of it, his dick is so long. Unabashedly, the God of Scarabs strokes himself while staring hungrily into my eyes. All I can think is that Tupac would definitely be enjoying this show ... *I am.*

Not to be outdone, Raiden shucks his pants *clear off* and stands fully naked in all his ninja-like glory. I blink a couple of times in shock since I kind of considered Raiden shy ... *I guess not.* Reserved might have been a better word, but he's clearly thrown *all his reservations* to the wind. And with one look at those pale washboard abs, I'm not about to protest. He picks me up effortlessly and I hook my legs around his waist.

We kiss for a long minute, his tongue stroking mine until I get lost in the sensation. Then I feel Khepri at my back, pressing into me with his chest and cock. For a moment, I just revel at being sandwiched between these two strong men, until Khepri decides to move this threesome along.

"You got the front and I got the back?" he asks Raiden and I feel my ass clench in trepidation—*and a little anticipation.*

"Gods, you are so unromantic," I lament and Raiden chuckles, tweaking a nipple through my shirt.

"We aren't Dev or Tupac—and that's part of why you're drawn to us, even if you won't admit it to yourself."

I grumble a bit at this, but know he's right. I'm drawn to both him and Khepri because they aren't trying to be gentle or tender like the other two men. They are raw, demanding—*consuming.*

"Don't worry about what we're doing, just enjoy the ride," Khepri murmurs, lifting my arms to remove my shirt slowly.

Raiden's hands follow, tracing up the now naked expanse of my sides to my breasts. My breath hitches when he cups them roughly and pinches my nipples while Khepri places biting kisses across the back of my shoulders.

Gently, I'm lowered to my feet and Raiden slowly

peels off my yoga pants. He works at an excruciatingly leisurely pace meant to tantalize me—*and it does*. By the time the two men have my leggings around my ankles, my pussy is throbbing with need.

It doesn't help that both their hot, hard cocks keep brushing the front and back of my thighs.

I can't stop the deep groan that escapes my mouth when Khepri reaches up and runs a finger along my pussy to my ass. There, he slips under my thong to explore me a little further. I immediately tense up—*no one has ever touched me there.*

"Don't ... don't you need some, ah, lube or something?" I pant since Raiden has joined Khepri in teasing me—except his fingers are buried deep inside my aching core, pumping in and out.

"I'm actually the god of secretions," Khepri announces and I collapse into Raiden, giggling.

"You seriously need some romantic pointers from Dev or Lover," I chortle. "The god of secretions! What the hell is wrong with you?!"

Even Raiden chuckles and Khepri joins in before explaining.

"I just meant that I've got you covered in the lube department."

"It's official—this has to be the world's most awkward threesome ever," I decide, but I don't care.

For some odd reason, it seems to be working for us —which is a testimony of how fucked up we are and this situation really is.

"We need more foreplay," Raiden demands.

"No one says that," Khepri tells him with an eye roll, still playing with my ass, gently circling my hole which, now, magically appears to be lubed. "And no one does foreplay anymore."

"Is that true?" Raiden asks me.

"Um ... I think it depends on the circumstances. I didn't really with Dev," I admit self-consciously, "but I didn't need it. But, I agree, maybe a little foreplay wouldn't hurt with us." Taking it slow might help alleviate my nerves, which are jangling like pennies in a pocket.

"See?" Raiden snorts at Khepri. "Ok, halfling, suck my cock."

Both Khepri and I stare at Raiden, waiting for him to grin or show he's teasing ...

He doesn't and I realize that he's not joking.

"Wow," Khepri says in my ear. "And you think I'm unromantic?"

"It is an honor to bless my dick with one's mouth," Raiden coaches sanctimoniously. "What would you have said?"

Khepri pauses for a moment to think.

"I would have told her to open her mouth like a bank account so I can deposit my dick in it—that's much more amorous."

I lean forward, torn between horror and fits of laughter at the absurdity of their thought processes. The movement brings me dangerously close to

Raiden's pulsing erection, the tip already glistening with pre-cum. The man is far too ridiculous by half, but I can't help myself when my tongue flicks out to taste his salty essence.

Raiden tenses and, then, moans at my actions. I straighten up before he does something truly ungentlemanly and shoves the entire thing down my throat.

"How about we take turns?" I suggest.

"We lick you and you lick us?" Khepri says with an eye waggle.

"Exactly, but for longer than just one lick," I add on.

"All I got was one lick," Raiden grumbles like a baby, but picks me up again as if I weigh nothing. Then he tilts me back into Khepri and bends forward, unceremoniously burying his face between my legs, making me squeal a little.

Khepri leans me against his chest while Raiden does dangerously delicious things to my pussy with his tongue—*he might not use it to form the right words, but he makes up for it tenfold with how he uses it on me now.* Khepri resumes his assplay—his form of foreplay—and before long, I'm crying out in desperation.

I need to come.

No sooner do I think this, than both Khepri and Raiden thrust their fingers into me at the same time and they tip me over the edge. I scream loudly as my nails dig into Raiden's shoulder blades. My orgasm makes my head spin like a pinwheel, and everything blurs for a bit, before the sensation slows and the room starts to come back into focus. It takes me a second to come down from my euphoric high but, when I do, I'm still a squirmy mess of need. Instead of sating me, the amazing orgasm just has me craving *more*.

"No more foreplay," I pant.

"Agreed," Khepri growls.

Raiden doesn't say anything, but straightens and then lowers me onto his cock. He kisses me deeply and I blush, tasting myself—which is a ridiculous reaction considering I'm having a threesome. Kung-Fu uses his massive muscles to bounce me up and down his thick erection several times. I get to run my hands over his tensing biceps and rigid back muscles, which are nearly as hot and hard as the dick inside me, before Raiden pulls me into his chest and spreads my ass cheeks in invitation to Khepri—who wastes no time positioning himself there and rubs his dick against me urgently.

"We'll go slowly," he promises, feeding the tip of his dick into my ass.

I breathe through the sensations bombarding my body. I've never felt so full. After a minute or so, Khepri's fully seated inside of me. Neither god moves and I grow antsy.

"Please, move," I beg breathlessly.

This stirs them into motion and, in perfect timing, they fuck me just like I long for—rough and fast. I feel both their chests rub against me, both their heartbeats pounding so quickly that my skin vibrates with the sensations of three different racing hearts. Their grunts and moans of pleasure make my mind melt into a puddle of hormones.

Need takes over every thought. I don't last more than two minutes. I convulse around them in an orgasm that makes my eyes cross; but they aren't anywhere near finished. Over and over, they thrust into my body in perfect synchronization; part of me wonders if Raiden cheats, because my nerves light up like the tiniest bolt of lightning is circling my clit, but the other part of me doesn't freaking care. I come twice more before both finally unleash inside of me.

We stand there a moment, catching our breath, before Raiden and Khepri gently pull out of me and place me on my slightly unstable legs.

"Now, that's how you worship a god," Khepri smirks down at me.

"I still say it's with my cock in her mouth," Raiden rejoins, but I can tell he's teasing.

His face is devoid of his previous anger and he reminds me of Concussed Raiden—*happier, freer.* I point this out and Khepri laughs.

"I guess all he needed was to get laid after all!"

AFTER I'VE SHOWERED AND CHANGED, I COME DOWN TO the kitchen for sustenance. A girl needs to be replenished after that many earth-shattering orgasms. Dev and Tupac are already there with Raiden and Khepri, doing gods know what on the computer. I hope my shower rinsed the lingering smell of … boning, but Khepri's lascivious smile tells me it didn't.

Thank the gods Dev and Lover don't have the same senses as gods. *I don't know if I could handle any more men in my life being able to sniff my big O's.*

"What are you four up to?"

"Hacking into different databases," Dev answers distractedly.

I let out a long-suffering sigh. "I hope you don't get caught," I worry and Dev sends me a tender, albeit disparaging, look.

"Babe—I'm the best hacker ever. No one is going to catch me. Besides, no human would care about what I'm doing."

That statement has my attention.

"Um, what does *that* mean?" I wonder nervously.

I worry about my Dev doing something so irrevocably stupid against any of the gods—he's too vulnerable and I can't lose him.

Dev grins at me and scratches at his beard before his fingers go wild at the keyboard.

"I'm just changing some of the information for the more well-known dickstain gods on sites such as Wikipedia and Encyclopedia Britannica. Nothing big, just little things to undermine their powers and make them a laughingstock to the rest of humanity. Right now, I'm writing about Zeus' fetish with bestiality, fucking as an animal. I wanted to make him impotent, but his eighty million kids refute that. Tupac and Khepri are helping me come up with things."

"Not you, Raiden?" I tease and Kung-Fu winces.

"It goes against how I was raised ... even if I now know these gods to be, ah, dickstains." He has trouble even saying the word.

I laugh at his admission when, suddenly, the brightly lit kitchen dims significantly. Frowning, I peek out a window and see a solar eclipse. I've only ever read about them. I take a second to marvel at the moon's dark shadow and the reddish ring that tinges the outside of the moon, which has obscured the sun. The others join me.

"Huh ... I don't recall reading anything about an upcoming solar eclipse," Dev says, scratching his head.

The others just shrug. They aren't human and don't know what's happening on Earth. I watch for a moment longer before going to the fridge and getting a bottle of water. I keep the lights off so everyone can enjoy the show outside. As I'm wondering how long the eclipse will last, I take a much needed swig of my water.

I'm seriously dehydrated—*a testimony to how strenuous threesomes can be.*

As the cooling liquid hits my tongue, my body sighs in relief—until it hits my taste buds. Instantly, I recognize the metallic flavor as blood.

Freaking gross!

I gag trying to spit it out. Lover rushes over to

smack my back as I choke, my body heaving against what my brain refuses to acknowledge—that I just drank fricking blood!

Dev turns on the lights and I hold up the bottle, the bright scarlet of its contents shining brightly from inside.

"It's blood!" I spit, rushing to the sink and turning it on so I can wash out my mouth, but, even there, the tap runs red.

Frantically, I wipe at my tongue, trying to dislodge the taste from my mouth while the others look on grimly.

"What the hell is going on?" I shriek in disgust and a little fear.

"I think that I know," Dev announces dourly. "Ra."

And just like that, the perfect bubble that I've been living in pops.

20

DEVIN

"Shit. I know what this is! I know what this is!" I mutter as I start to pace.

The pieces fall together in my head, just like lines of code. The eclipse, water turning to blood ... I rack my brain as I try to think of what's next.

"Dev?" Val comes over and strokes my hand.

I grab both her hands and cup them inside mine.

"It's the plagues of Egypt!"

"What?" Tupac and Raiden ask simultaneously as they stare out the window.

"The plagues! The curses that came over Egypt!" I turn to Val. "I had to do a report when I was in third grade. Egypt was struck down by ten plagues. They thought it was a curse."

Khepri grimaces. "That's what happens when you piss off Ra. He goes mental. Always taking it to the extreme." He marches to the front door and opens it.

He steps outside and stares up at the sky. All of us follow him.

Val clutches at my t-shirt, worry filling her gorgeous eyes.

"What are the plagues?"

"They're environmental phenomena that—"

"No! Literally, what are they?"

She spins me around and points at a mass in the sky approaching us quickly. With the eclipse, it's hard to make out whatever it is, other than it's *alive*.

"Um ..."

Panic makes my brain short circuit for a second. I close my eyes to block out the sight of impending doom.

I hear a sizzle. My eyes shoot open as next to me, Raiden lets loose a bolt of lightning. It streaks through the sky toward the mass and lights up ... a giant, moving hill of—

"Frogs!" Val shrieks and shoves me in front of her.

I didn't realize she was scared of frogs. The stupid thought passes through my head instead of the obvious, better thought: *what the fuck are we going to do about them?*

"I can fry them?" Raiden offers. He puts his hand up to send out another bolt of lightning, but Val stops him.

"Can we just ... I don't know, hide inside?" she whispers. "I hate to kill those innocent but nasty, disgusting, slimy—"

"You don't like frogs?" Khepri asks.

222

She shudders.

Tupac moves close and wraps an arm around her as I feel a whip sting my forearm and wrap around it. I turn back to see a giant bullfrog's tongue encircling my wrist like a bangle. The frog itself is barreling toward me like a squishy, oversized, mucus-coated marshmallow of doom.

I smack it as soon as it reaches me and it flies away only to come reeling right back in like one of those kids' paddle balls. I smack it a second time and try to frantically unravel its tongue on my arm before it comes sailing back again.

Next to me, Val shrieks as a chunk of the frog-mass breaks away. I watch in horror as a hundred frogs land on Khepri at once, covering him head to toe. One of them even has teeth and I hear him roar in outrage and pain as it bites down on his cheek. Another's tongue darts into his mouth.

Oh, hell no.

I'm not kissing any frogs—no matter what the fairy tales say. Val's my happily ever after.

Val's fear starts to make sense as Khepri falls and even more frogs hop over to cover him. Luckily, he has his powers. He transforms into a scarab and flies out from underneath the frog pile.

Behind him, the huge mass of frogs undulates closer. It's like 'The Blob,' but a living, croaking, tongue-whipping version.

I turn to check on Val, just in time to see a frog land

in her hair. She screams and instantly transforms into her swan.

I'm distracted by the graceful curve of her neck, the beauty of her wings, the sensuous snap of her beak—

She decapitates the frog and then flies right for another.

"Yeah girl! Shake your tail feathers!" Tupac cheers her on.

I watch her arch through the sky, orange lightning shooting from her beak and electrocuting the frogs closest to us, making their legs seize up and their little bodies pop as they cook like popcorn. She's magnificent.

It's only when Raiden accidentally stumbles into me that I realize I've started stroking myself through my pants at the sight.

"Fucking Aphrodite!" I mutter. I wrench my gaze away from Val and punch each of the other three. "The love curse bullshit is distracting us. Val could get hurt!" I tell them.

Immediately, Raiden conjures up a jagged bolt of lightning and throws it at the giant swollen hill of frogs. It rushes through the air faster than Val can fly and hits that mass of frogs, bouncing from one to the next until they are all sizzling and the meadow around us smells like a barbecue in the bayou.

"Everybody, inside!" I gesture toward the tiny house that Thor built. We all run, and Val transforms back to a human (thank goodness because those epicly sexy swan legs and webbed toes were about to do me in) before she tumbles inside.

I slam the door shut behind her, my chest heaving, more from anxiety than the run. "We need a fucking plan."

"Well, I'm willing to take her mouth, and you all could rochambeau for her pussy—" Tupac starts.

I hold up a hand in his face. "Not a plan for *fucking*, idiot! A fucking plan to deal with what's going on outside!"

I glance around at the two gods. "How are we going to kick Ra's ass?"

Khepri straightens his shoulders and stares out the window at the mass of blackened, smoking frogs on the far side of the meadow. "Ra will only concede in honorable battle. He's very attached to the traditional ways of the gods. When I first wanted to divest myself of the thankless task of rolling the sun through Duat, I had to challenge Ra formally for his position. I had to act like I didn't want to step down, but ascend the throne. It was the only honorable way he could take my powers."

I stare at Khepri, my mouth falling open. Of the three of them, I'd always thought he was more sensible than the two droolers. Tupac was too in lust after years of deprivation to have much left in the way of brain cells. And Raiden ... well that knock on the head had left him with a screw or two loose. But this plan? This plan? I couldn't believe how idiotic it sounded.

I stomped through the foyer, underneath the hull of the twinkle-light boat. I smashed my hand into a wall in frustration. "Challenge Ra to direct combat? When you've already lost once? That seems like a great fucking idea."

Tupac raises a hand in the air. "Can you please stop using the word fucking?" He gestures down at his dick. The sun on his underpants is currently at least seven inches away from his body. "I can't help my reaction when I hear that word."

Khepri takes a long, hard look at Val. Then he marches forward, swoops her down into a dip, and kisses her. He stands her back up and stomps right out the front door into the meadow, which is swarming with flies? Gnats? Both? I'm not sure.

But that's the next plague. Bugs.

Khepri bats them away and spits heavily as he stalks through the long grass. I watch him through the window, a sense of foreboding settling into my stomach.

Next to me Raiden says, "That fool is going to get himself killed."

"Yup." Tupac agrees.

Val's hand flies to her mouth and I turn to see tears shining in her eyes. She doesn't want to lose Khepri. It would hurt her.

I swallow hard and turn to the guys. "Yeah, the shit-head's gonna die. Unless we help him."

21

VAL

Khepri walks outside, back straight, with all the confident arrogance I've come to hate about gods. But in this case, he's using that arrogance to protect the rest of us, and my heart swells a little inside my chest. I've never seen arrogance so misguidedly sweet.

Gods can't be killed, but the consequences for their feuds can sometimes be even worse.

I mean, technically, in Norse tradition, Odin killed Ymir and the earth was made out of Ymir's body and his brains are the clouds. That makes all of us on earth little cannibalistic parasites.

Zeus locked up Prometheus for giving fire to mortals and commissioned a bird to eat the poor guy's liver every day for all eternity. That doesn't even get into the long list of Ra's transgressions throughout history.

God punishments aren't half-hearted. Though, I

guess technically they could be. The winning god could have the losing god's heart ripped in half again and again.

The thought of anything happening to Khepri makes me feel as though a sword point is at my chest. I couldn't survive if something happened to him.

I yank open the door and scream, "Wait! Khepri! Don't!"

A huge pile of shit falls from the sky, like an avalanche, or a mudslide. It lands on the porch and shoves the front door closed, piling up until it's six feet high and has blocked the door completely.

I slam my fist into the door. "NO!"

I run to the side and stare out the tiny window next to the door, watching as one of the men I love marches toward his doom.

My heart gives a frail beat. But that kicks up into a panicked flutter as I spot Khepri's opponent.

From the edge of the treeline, Ra emerges. He's in his traditional mythological form today, a falcon head set on his shoulders, with a snake encircling a miniature sun on his head. He holds a string in one hand that floats up into the sky and disappears behind the shadowy moon. He pulls the string taught and the sun and moon hop forward in the sky. He's got the sun on a string, like a balloon, the lazy fuck. His beak opens and he gives a loud screech when he sees Khepri walk toward him.

I claw at the windows, my nails raking down the glass.

This is a bad idea—a horrible idea.

If Ra convinces Khepri to shapeshift, I'm certain that his falcon head could chomp Khepri's beetle-bug in two.

"Ok, so we should pool our resources," Dev says behind me.

But it's hard to focus on his words when I see Khepri bow to the asshole sun god. Ra shouldn't get to be a sun god. He should be the god of raw food, or minor abrasions, or inexperience … any of those would fit him better than powerful as fuck sun god. If he was any of those things, Khepri would stand a better chance of winning.

Ra lets out a shriek that makes my hair stand on end.

The hammer! I tear through the house, nearly upending a dining chair as I speed past the table to my room. I yank open my door and chest heaving, I call for Mjoli, where he's laying on the ruffled decorative pillow next to mine.

Mjoli doesn't stir from his spot, where he creates a deep divot, all snuggled in. It almost looks like he's sleeping. *How can he sleep at a time like this?*

I leap onto the bed and bounce before I lean forward I wrap my hand around the handle. I yank.

But Mjoli doesn't budge.

"What the hell?" I growl as I lean forward and grab the handle with both hands.

But the hammer might as well be welded to my bed frame. Because it won't move.

I try three more times before I collapse forward, hands falling to my lap as I start to sob. My chest twists so tight that it cracks.

Khepri is out there and in danger, trying to kill a god he's lost to before ... and the fucking hammer won't even move to let me help him?

"Why?" I scream at the inanimate object. "Why?"

A voice answers, "Because you would dishonor his sacrifice."

I turn to see Raiden standing in my door. I hold my arms out toward him and he walks forward. He takes a seat next to me and pulls me into a tender hug. His touch soothes my agitation away, the way a breeze breaks the heat on a midsummer day.

A tear streaks down my cheek and a sob gets stuck in my throat, making me cough.

Raiden rocks me gently, his hand smoothing down my back. "We will help him, Val. But you do not need your father's power. Your incredible cygnus form ..." He shudders even as he speaks, as if even imagining my swan form causes him intense pleasure. He swallows hard and pulls back slightly so he can look me in the eyes. His dark gaze is serious. "But we should hurry. Before the arrogant shit gets himself—"

I nod and stand, effectively cutting him off.

Raiden helps me up and walks me back through the house to where Dev and Tupac have armed themselves with household objects: a fireplace poker, an umbrella, a small lamp with a gold shade, and the smartest choice — a kitchen knife.

I run back to the window to peer outside. The breath leaves my lungs when I see Ra has Khepri in a headlock and my handsome god has blood dripping from his mouth. His eyes meet mine for a split second before I see Ra raise a huge dagger.

Fuck!

I'm rabid. I'm frantic. I slam my hand against the door. I scream, "Raiden, wind now! Use wind. Break wind! Break the damn door!"

Raiden lifts his hand and hurricane level winds blast the door and the pile of shit in front of it.

The door slowly opens and we all burst through.

22

KHEPRI

ADMITTEDLY, I'M GETTING MY ASS HANDED TO ME BY RA. Before, I let him win because it was part of my plan to help Nut. Now, I *need* to win for this new plan to succeed—one where I humiliate Ra by kicking his butt in one-on-one combat.[1]

The Greeks emulated us and built huge amphitheaters to host their ass-kickings. In fact, I'm fairly certain that modern-day wrestling stems from what Ra and I are doing right now—except, it's not fake. I'm not over here pulling punches like Samoa Joe.[2] And Ra might be a pretty boy, but he packs a mean punch.

I duck just as he throws another fist at my face, his expression the foulest scowl—which is hard to see with an eclipsed sun and a swarm of gnats.

Ra hates traitors and I hate little bitches—so our anger is probably pretty mutual at this point.

I swipe at his side and he jumps back.

"You deceitful betrayer! You are a smear on the good name of sun gods! A shadow! A blight!" he screams in ancient Egyptian.

I snort and throw a shitball at his face—*a really gloppy one*.

"That's fucking rich since every sun god is a conniving dick!"

I take great satisfaction when Ra takes my crap to his face.

Behind me, I hear a giant BOOM and I turn briefly to see the others running toward me—Val and Tupac leading the pack. I groan. If they intervene now, Ra will never stop attacking them! They will have violated what he considers sacred combat.

I spin back to Ra, who is frantically trying to dislodge semi-liquefied poop from his nostrils.

"I take it back—almost every sun god is a conniving dick, but I know a good one. This one is for him."

Before Ra can blink, I throw a right hook that he never saw coming (he's got shit for eyes, right now). I can be a mean bastard, too, when needed. I punch him three more times across the jaw. The fucker is strong— I'll give him that—all he does is stagger back a bit, but he doesn't fall once.

"Those were for Tupac, Raiden, Val, and all the other demis."

I wait for my words to register; then, I rush him

hard, tackling his midsection and bringing him to the ground. I raise my fist, intent on knocking out the cosmic cumstain.

"And this one is for Nut, the Demigodling, and *me!*"

But, just as I'm about to lower my fist, Ra lets out a burst of blinding light—and when I say *blinding*, I *mean* blinding. Just like that, I can't see a thing, which is bad because last time I checked, Ra still had a death dagger in his hands.

How is a death dagger different from a regular dagger, you might ask; well, let me tell you. A regular dagger just makes normal puncture wounds in its victim—perfectly harmless in the long-run if you are a god (which I am). BUT, a death dagger is a weapon specifically crafted by *all* the gods of death—that's a shit-ton of gods, too. They're like sun gods or rabbits; they just keep multiplying. This dagger can strip the immortality from a god, making it my number one goal *not* to get stabbed by it.

I yell for the others to stay back, even though I can't see what I'm doing. I fumble blindly, my hands trying to reach for Ra as my thoughts race.

Val lost her immortality when she lost her virginity and Dev is equally vulnerable. Ra could kill them with a flick of his dagger or a minor solar flare.

Tupac is just a demi and Raiden is a hot-headed fool who will end up stabbed quicker than he can blink.

Fuck—*I* am the only one equipped enough to fight

Ra! The others weren't supposed to leave the safety of Thor's house!

Too late, I can feel them at my back, dragging me away from the fight. I hear the hot sizzle of electricity arcing in the air and I know Raiden and Val are giving Ra a dose of his own medicine.

I hear the sun god scream in agony. But I don't even feel an ounce of satisfaction.

His agony was supposed to come from me.

I'm furious that they took my fight from me. But underneath that fury is a deep layer of self-loathing. I was losing. They know it. I know it. Ashamed, I hang my head and wait for my vision to clear. I was supposed to defeat Ra—it was my only goal and I failed.

"Khep—are you ok, man?" Dev asks in a shaky whisper near my left ear.

"Ra blinded me. It's temporary, but I can't see a thing." I choke out the words, feeling as small and useless as a child.

"Shit, that's not good," he mutters. "We need a different plan." Dev says this last part mostly to himself.

"Tupac, get Val and Raiden! Meet us back in the house! Fucking hurry!"

"I don't like to fuck in a rush—" Tupac starts.

"TUPAC!" Dev roars.

"Sheesh, can't anyone take a sex joke around here? I'm going; I'm going."

"Just run with me, I'll get you in the house," Dev directs and I follow his lead.

All is well until I slam into the door jamb. Even though I can't see, red lines flash across my eyes as I knock myself nearly unconscious. Fuck—I've had my ass handed to me by Ra and a door casing today. That's ... *sad*.

"Khepri! Fuck, man! Sorry. Here—this way," Dev apologizes.

I rub my forehead sardonically.

"Remind me to never have you lead me anywhere again," I tell Dev wryly as he successfully—*this time*—leads me inside of the safe house.

Just as spots begin to dance before my eyes and my vision slowly returns, the other three join us and I breathe a sigh of relief.

Thank fuck everyone's ok—that *Val's* ok. My eyes travel down her form and I realize her bra strap has slipped down. I lean forward and right it gently for her, dragging my fingers lightly over her shoulder.

I apologize for my failure with my look, but not words. It's too painful to say aloud, plus, I'm not sure she could respond yet. Both Raiden and she are panting heavily.

I'm not the only one to notice.

"Sounds like you two were getting it on hard core," Tupac comments with an eye-waggle.

"DUDE!" Dev admonishes. "Focus—for one freaking minute! Think about an orgy *after* we've

237

defeated Ra. That is—if we defeat him. We need a new plan. Sorry, Khep, but your ass almost got stabbed too many times for you to do this on your own. We're a team."

"Dev's right," Val agrees, crossing her arms.

My head drops and I feel her disapproval like a slap.

"About the orgy?" Tupac wonders hopefully and we all shove him. "What?! Was it something I said?"

"Ugh. You're such a little horndog," Val laughs at him.

"Hey! My horndog is not little, thank you very much!" Tupac counters.

"Oh, go jack off in the corner while the adults discuss important shit," Dev snaps.

"Calm down, everyone. Tu—keep your dick in your banana hammock. Ra is still outside and I don't really want to test my dad's wards on this house. And I was saying that Dev's right that *we need to work as a team*."

She gives Tupac a pointed look and he deflates a little at her lack of orgy talk.

"Khepri—what was that dagger Ra had? Some ritual Egyptian slicer 'n dicer?"

"Death dagger," I grit out.

I feel like someone beat the crap out of me—FYI, *Ra didn't*. He just got in some lucky punches. Oh, and the door jamb got in a good smack to my forehead, too.

Raiden inhales sharply at my announcement.

"Erm … what's the difference between a regular dagger and a death dagger?" Dev wonders.

Now, you understand why I explained earlier. Humans think a knife is a dagger is a sword is an equally lethal weapon.

Wrong.

I explain to Dev just why a death dagger is so dangerous to a god.

"Does that mean it's not hazardous to me?" he asks.

Humans are so cute in their naivety.

"No, stupid. It just means it kills you instantly," Raiden answers in his usual tactful manner—*not*.

"So, this dagger can render *any* god mortal?" Val queries, chewing on that delicious bottom lip of hers.

"Any god," I confirm.

"Even Ra?"

I pause as her words sink into my head and watch as an idea begins to form in hers.

"Yeah ... *even* Ra," I verify.

"Then, we need to stab him with his own dagger."

"And I can barbeque his ass, afterward," Raiden finishes triumphantly.

"I'm not so sure your lightning power will be enough to subdue him long enough. His solar power helps mitigate the damage your electricity can do," I caution.

"Can we stab him again with the dagger?" Val suggests.

"Sure ... if you're lucky enough to get in another shot," I snort.

"Well, we are," Val states. "And I'm infusing the second stabbing with my Valkyrie powers."

"You're going to turn him into a swan?" Dev asks in confusion.

Raiden grins evilly.

"No—*she's going to kill him.*"

23

VAL

"Exactly," I confirm. "I'm going to infuse death into the, ah, death dagger. Wow, that sounds super redundant."

Dev chuckles.

"I smell what you're stepping in," he says.

"What's that mean?" Raiden asks Tupac.

"It means she's stepping in shit and he can smell it," Tupac explains.

Raiden and Khepri wrinkle their noses.

"Humans are weird," Kung-Fu tells Khepri.

"Do the shit jokes never end?" Khepri laments with a shake of his head.

"Guys—problem," Dev pipes up.

"What?" I ask, already on edge.

"We haven't solved the sun problem yet. What are we going to do about the sun if we succeed in actually killing Ra? It's going to drop and destroy all of humanity—we're goners regardless!"

Tupac carefully clears his throat. "I know that you all only view me as good for fucking, but I have other talents. Namely, solar ones."

Dev looks at him skeptically. "But didn't you already … um … try that?"

Raiden snorts. "Yes. He was an epic failure."

I shoot both of them a reprimanding look. "Not helping." I turn to Tupac and run my hand down his thick bicep. His sun rises in response. I step closer. He just needs confidence to access and better control his powers. Just like I always did.

I rub against his hard on slightly and say, "You fantastical horndog! You can catch the fiery ball in the sky!"

I think my tactic works, because he says, "Don't let it ever be said that Lover can't catch some balls!" with a dirty grin.

"Ok, Raiden—you're on winds. I'll transform into my swan and sizzle Ra's ass. Khepri—toss him as much shit as you can. Between the three of us, we should be able to distract him enough to get the dagger and stab him a couple of times. Tupac, be on the lookout for this because the sun is coming down. Everyone, put your hands in!"

Tupac grins and places his hand on top of mine. Khepri and Raiden look confused, but follow suit. I wait for Dev to join, but hear him politely clear his voice, instead.

"Aren't you forgetting someone, Val?" he asks.

"What? No. I'm waiting for you, goof. Get your hand in here!"

"I mean—what am I doing to fight Ra?"

"Oh, um ..."

I trail off weakly.

Dev is different. He isn't a fighter like Raiden and Khepri and he can't catch the sun like Tupac—not that he isn't talented and special—I just don't want to risk him getting stabbed by Ra. As Khepri explained, it would likely be fatal. I know I'm being hypocritical since I'm equally mortal, but being a demi and having swan powers gives me an advantage that he doesn't have.

I don't know what I would do if I lost Dev. But, I can see by his wounded look how much I've hurt him with my hesitation.

"How's your throwing arm?" I ask him.

"Um ... I played tee-ball," he offers.

"Awesome!" I crow with a big smile at him. "You're going to help distract Ra. Throw anything and everything you can at him—but for fuck's sake, stay out of his way. All of you!"

Dev smiles and nods, and I sigh in relief. This time, he sticks his hand on top of mine stacked on Raiden's, Khepri's, and Tupac's.

"Two, four, six, eight—who are we going to obliterate? RA!" The three gods gaze blankly as I lift my hand and cheer.

Dev scrunches his nose up. "I only played ball for a year but that's not how I remember that going ... isn't it 'two, four, six, eight—who do we appreciate' and, then, you say the other team's name in a show of good sportsmanship?"

I throw my arms up in exasperation.

"Ugh! You've all ruined my pep rally and, yes, Dev—but we aren't 'appreciating' Ra, we're trying to kill him. Remember?"

"Right, sorry."

Just then, the house is flooded with bright piercing light. It's white and feels invasive.

"Ra," Khepri grits out.

"Come out, come out, wherever you are!" sings a taunting voice outside of the safety of our Thor-warded home.

"Go fuck yourself, go fuck yourself, wherever you are!" Raiden rejoins in a thunderous voice.

The rest of us stare at him in shock.

"What?" he wonders.

"That was ..." I start.

"Hot," Tupac finishes, giving Raiden a thorough once over, making the Japanese weather god frown.

"I'm not hot. I'm powerful," he corrects.

"You can be both," I soothe, though personally, I agree with Tupac's assessment. Raiden's angry yell was alpha-hot. "Now, let's go kick some Rass—that's Ra-Ass combined."

Khepri shakes his head, chuckling. "Right, it's Rass killing time."

We line up shoulder to shoulder and Khepri slowly opens the door as my heart starts a hopping techno beat inside my chest.

This time, when we burst from the house, it's not in a panic, but as a cohesive unit with a single purpose: to bring Rass down.

Immediately, Raiden blasts Ra with a gale force enough to flatten a small town. Ra takes the assault well, standing even as he's blown backward a few feet across the meadow.

Ra raises his hands and I expect fire to come shooting our way. Instead, I hear a distant lowing, that rapidly becomes louder. A dull thump in the grass becomes a stampede. Seconds later, cows from the surrounding farms burst through the trees and into the meadow. Their eyes glow green, like they're possessed. In the trees behind them, squirrels with glowing green eyes chatter at us from the trees.

Dev stage whispers, "The fourth and fifth plagues!"

Tupac shoots a fireball at the nearest cow. "Cookout!" he yells. "How do you like your steak?"

"Definitely not still mooing," Dev replies.

The other cows rush at Tupac, but he creates a fire circle around us, keeping the possessed animals at bay.

Raiden starts to jolt the bovines who test the fire circle with lightning.

The squirrels launch an aerial assault. They leap from the trees, sailing down at my guys with furious little warrior shrieks that I didn't know squirrels could make. Dev opens his umbrella and uses it as a shield to knock away the squirrels and keep them outside the circle.

I shift into my cygnus form and take to the air, my wings lifting me easily and maneuvering like I've been flying all my life.

I keep my eyes on Ra. I'm filled with fury just at the sight of him, but I cage that rage, trap it with concentration and focus. I open my beak and let orange lightning zap out at the insufferable man who oppressed demis for so long—who planned to kill us all simply because we were part human.

Ra doesn't take our attack lying down. He raises his hand, calling forth more light. That asshole's gonna try to blind us again? *Sorry, Ra, get a new party trick.*

I close my eyes in time not to be blinded, and I hope the others had the foresight to do so, as well. When I open my eyes again, Ra isn't in the same spot. I look for his creepy-ass falcon head and find it in direct combat with Khepri—again.

Ra's beak snaps at Khepri but Khepri fills it with shit before shoving it to one side and punching Ra in the neck. In response, Ra sweeps a leg across Khepri's legs. Khepri falls to the ground but raises his hand and

I see a huge lump form in the back of Ra's pants as the sun god gives a shriek.

I'm guessing that shit hurt. Literally.

Thankfully, Bi-Polar seems to be holding his own better this time. They tussle for a bit longer before Ra pulls out his death dagger and lunges for my shit god. Khepri twirls away, but Ra just dances closer.

That ratchets up my fear. I can't let that dagger touch my Khepri.

Raiden and I up our attacks, shooting lightning at the crazed animals, but also attempting to get closer to Ra.

Ra is solely focused on Khepri. That is, until a rock slams into the side of his right temple with a sickening crack. It makes the sun god's bird head twist to an unnatural angle.

Startled, everyone stops fighting and looks over to see ... Dev, standing in the middle of Tupac's ring of fire with a handful of stones and a mean fucking glare stamped on his face.

What a total badass, I think. *No! Focus, Val!*

I turn my attention back to Ra, who has already recovered. He sends out a pulse of fire that makes all the guys duck and I have to pump my wings hard to escape it. I feel the flames licking at my webbed feet and singing my tail feathers. That both scares me and pisses me the fuck off. I push harder to get out of range and then renew my fighting attempts.

I send orange lightning at the sun fucker but that

round disk on his head acts as a lightning rod and attracts my bolt. It doesn't even seem to faze the asshole.

In fact, it feels like we all double our efforts, but the harder we fight, the more crazed the cows get. Several end up standing on their hind legs and barrelling right through Tupac's ring of fire.

"Holy shit! Talk about mad cows!" he exclaims. "Come on, Bessie! Bring it on!" Tupac seems to relish the challenge.

I rip my eyes away from them. They can handle some heifers, but Ra is the true threat.

I turn back to Ra and Khepri. That's when I see Ra stagger. Khepri kicks at the sun god's hand, trying to dislodge the dagger. That brilliant piece of shit succeeds—Ra's fingers bend backward and the weapon goes flying.

"Raiden! Quick, blow the dagger to me!" I honk, belatedly realizing that all I'm doing is sending lightning into the air because I'm a swan and can't talk—but I can bark electricity; so, there's that, I guess.

Ra shoves Khepri away and dives for his precious death dagger, but Khep isn't going down without a fight. He yanks Ra's ankle and the sun god goes down —straight into a steamy pile of dung that Khepri conjures up out of nowhere. Ra's inhuman screech makes me cringe. I think he just got a mouthful of crap.

Ew. But totally well-deserved.

"Eat shit!" my shit-god yells.

Unfortunately, Khepri hid the dagger under said pile of poop and Ra is over Khep's bullshit. He ignores his beakful of dung, shoves a hand right in the middle of the impressive fecal mass and triumphantly pulls the death dagger free.

My wings hold me aloft but my heart plummets when I see the weapon in his hand. Khepri doesn't see it yet. And I can't warn him in my swan form. I can't talk.

I open my beak and shoot impotent lighting at Ra, knowing it won't hurt him, but unable to *just* watch.

Viciously, Ra stabs the death-infused tip into the side of my god of bowel movements.

Ra might as well have stabbed me because my heart rips painfully knowing how vulnerable Khepri is now. I watch the transformation come over Khepri as he changes from god to mortal. There's a glow under his skin that fades. The confident smirk he normally wears turns into thin-lipped desperation.

"NO!" I scream mentally.

Khepri swivels out of Ra's grasp, dislodging the blade from his side, even though the weapon remains in the tight grip of our enemy.

I see a thin stream of blood well up and spill over from Khepri's wound and tears prick my eyes as the reality is driven home—Khepri's no longer immortal. The dagger in Ra's hand worries me. My second worry is that Ra isn't even going to have to stab him again to kill him—the man's going to die of infection from being punctured by a dagger covered in shit!

All that worry churns in my stomach like sewage and I feel sick.

Ra swipes at Khepri, who dodges but groans in pain. I honk and shoot lightning at the few remaining crazed cows to vent my fury because I feel like my wings are tied, my power is useless to hurt the sun god.

How the hell are we going to kill him?

My despair turns to hope when I see Raiden stealthily come up behind Ra and hook his left arm across the sun god's throat.

Fucking yes! I want to fist pump but end up doing an awkward aerial flip that makes me dizzy.

Ra's falcon head squawks in protest as he fights against the strong Japanese god. Raiden uses a series of body blows and then a flying kick to send Ra sprawling limply. As the sun god screeches and climbs to his feet, Khepri uses Ra's distraction to yank the death dagger out of the sun god's hand. He flips it over and quickly pierces Ra in his big toe.

Haha yes! Now the motherfucker has one foot in the grave!

If we ever make it out of this alive, I'm sure we'll all give Khep hell for where he finally managed to stab Ra but, right now, I'm just grateful that he succeeded.

We did it—we stripped Ra of his immortality!

Now, the bastard is just as vulnerable as the rest of us.

The anger and fear simmering on his bird face confirms that Ra knows this, too. With a vicious squawk he runs forward and head-butts my weather god in the forehead—hard. Raiden sways, but manages to stay on his feet—a testimony to how hard-headed the god is.

In a move almost too swift for my eyes to perceive, Ra reaches down and removes the dagger from his toe. Apparently, he can move at the speed of light even as a mortal.

Khepri hurtles toward Ra from behind, ready to kick him in the ass—literally—but Ra swiftly rises and pivots in one smooth movement ...

And shoves the blade deep into Khepri's heart.

No!

I gasp in shock and denial, dropping from the sky to land on my ass in human form. The meadow grass and a cow separate me from him, so I struggle to my feet, tears already forming in my now-human eyes.

"Khepri!" I cry.

His eyes lock on mine, showing the same surprise and, then, *POOF*—motherfucking *poof*—he's gone. The death dagger in his side disappears with him.

I start to shake in rage and utter desolation.

"You bastard," I seethe at Ra, not caring a whit about his powers as I stomp over to the short Egyptian, who's wearing a triumphant smile on his face. My vision goes red and my breathing speeds up. Adrenaline courses through me and my pulse pounds in my ears.

No. Ra won't win today. I won't allow it.

I plan on killing the fucker with my bare hands, when I hear Dev shout my name. I turn to look at him before I get within Ra's reach. My bestie is running full speed at me—with an odd and deadly-looking arrow in his hand.

"Now, Val! Now!"

It takes me a second to realize what he wants, but when he launches himself in the air in an impressive acrobatic feat, I realize his intent—as does Ra.

Dev's gonna use that motherfucker to cut the bitch.

Something stirs within me. The inklings that I've had before, about death, play through my mind in a flash, fanning out like playing cards so that I can see each one. And I realize something about myself that I never knew. Those inklings are possibilities, options, just like cards in one's hand. And I get to choose to put them into play.

I get to choose who lives or dies.

All this flashes through me in less than a moment as Dev ninjas his way through the air. I lift my hands and I pour my soul into that arrow, infusing it with the age-old death powers of my Valkyrie roots and a prayer of retribution for my shit god; then, I watch that arrow find its home exactly where Ra deserves—in his black heart, in the same spot that he stabbed Khepri.

Ra screams and convulses, his falcon head shifting back into his human one. He drops to his knees, blood pouring copiously from his chest. His glassy eyes glare at Dev and me, and he attempts to garble out—what I assume is—a curse. But, before he exact his revenge and Egyptian-style voodoo, Raiden leans up and grasps the side of Ra's head, twisting it to the side in a move I swear I've only seen in movies.

With a sickening crunch, Raiden snaps Ra's neck and the sun god goes down, down, down ...

As does the sun.

The eclipse stops. But not because the sun has moved past the moon. Because the sun is sinking below it.

My stomach drops as the familiar form in the sky literally plummets toward the Earth. I glance back at Ra and see a rope, which had been invisible while he was alive. Now, as the sun falls, the rope is rapidly coiling up beside him, as though Ra had been dragging the sun through the sky like a helium balloon.

"Oh shit, oh shit, oh shit," I moan. This is exactly what we feared—exactly what Tupac practiced for— but that practice had been disastrous.

"Tupac's got this," Dev whispers, and I pray that he's right.

I know that all of humanity only has seconds left to live and I send my love to my dad, to Raiden, to Dev, to Lover, and especially to my brave shithead, Khepri, who gave everything for us.

As the sun's heat surrounds me, my hope fades and this final thought flickers through my head: *I'm finally going to join my mom and Dot but, honestly, I want more time with my men.*

The world goes dark and I close my eyes, but instead of imminent death, there's ... nothing.

Wow.

The afterlife is super shitty.

Then, everything grows bright again and I realize that I'm not dead, nor is the Earth destroyed—*because Tupac is holding the sun between his shoulders much like Atlas holds the world!*

That sweet, sweet horndog has quadrupled in size to hold the massive ball of fire. I watch in awe, amazed that he can shoulder the weight and not get burnt to a sexy-ass crisp.

"Hold on—I'm going to get Atum," Raiden announces, and before I can protest, he winks out of existence.

"Who's Atum?" I wonder.

Dev tiredly pulls his phone from his back pocket and looks it up. "Another Egyptian sun god."

"Fuck—how many are there?!" I roll my eyes. Dev shrugs, clearly exhausted.

I can only imagine what it was like for Khepri, being one of many, when gods are supposed to be so fucking special. He was special ... to me. My throat closes up and I have to change the direction of my thoughts. I ask, "Dev, where'd you get that arrow?"

The sweetest man that I know turns beet red and

looks away, but not before I catch the look of shame on his face.

"Dev?" I prod when he maintains his silence.

He heaves a heavy sigh.

"It's ... from Aphrodite's demigod son," he confesses.

"The Greek god of love?" I clarify.

Dev nods. "It's a love arrow."

"Why would you need a love arrow?!" I ask incredulously. Jealousy starts to eat away at the sadness inside. Who was he going to use that arrow on?

"Because ... I thought it would be the only way you would ever, ah, love me, I guess," he answers uncomfortably, running a hand across his beard.

I blink at the man—*how could he be so blind and clueless?*

I LEAN OVER AND KISS DEV WITH ALL THE LOVE I HAVE for him in my heart—he returns it tenfold and I feel like the luckiest woman in the universe.

Suddenly, Raiden reappears out of thin air, pop up storm clouds surrounding him. Next to him is a man who could be Ra's twin.

I recoil, but Raiden rushes to explain,"This is Atum. He's a good guy—another deity whose powers were consumed by Ra's greed. He's willing to take back on his solar duties and alleviate Tupac of the chore."

"Heck yeah, get this sweaty galactical ballsac off my back," Tupac booms.

Atum snorts, "It is not a chore, but a great honor!"

Raiden rolls his eyes at me and winks. "That's what I meant, sorry."

A chuckle wells up inside of me at the Japanese god's words and antics because he knows that he used to sound just like Atum!

The Egyptian god disappears to—I assume—take the sun

It lurches in the sky, rays burning brighter for a moment.

Seconds later, Tupac slowly shrinks back down to normal size and joins us in a heap on the ground. I straddle him, hugging him fiercely.

"Woah—are we having our orgy now that I'm not hung like a fucking giant?" he jokes.

Unexpectedly, instead of laughing, like his words intended, I burst into tears. "Khepri's dead!" I wail inconsolably. My heart feels like someone's taken Mjoli to it and pounded relentlessly, like they were tenderizing meat. I'm smooshed inside.

And nothing can undo a smooshed heart.

As if the heavens feel my pain, rain begins to fall from the sky—except, I realize that there are no clouds and it's not rain, but ...

Pieces of shit.

One particular clump lands in my hands. I squeal in disgust and drop it, but Raiden scoops it up without hesitation. He digs inside of the little ball of dung until he pulls out ...

"A worm?" I say with a cringe.

Gross. Shit worms. Maggots. I'm about to gag. I cover my mouth in disgust. Now, I've seen it all, but Dev gets a big, excited smile on his face.

"No! It's a dung beetle larvae!"

"What?" I ask in confusion but Raiden and Tupac seem to understand what Dev is trying to say.

Their faces split into huge grins.

"What is going on?" I cry out.

"My best friend came back," Raiden answers, in his mock-concussed voice and holding up the wriggling little worm.

Though we became mortal, we didn't lose our powers. Khepri created himself out of nothing. He can recreate himself out of nothing.

My hand falls away from my mouth and my jaw drops. Just like *that*, my world is right again.

My crappy god has reincarnated himself!

24

TUPAC

Twenty-Four Hours, Eight Minutes, and Seventeen Seconds Later ...

Yes—*motherfucking orgy time!*

I slap my hands and rub them together in glee. "This is gonna be so dope!"

I bob my head side to side to music only I can hear —the lyrics of *I Wanna Sex You Up* making my hips pump to the rhythm.

"We need candles," Raiden insists as he helps me pick up a cooler and take it outside, but I shake my head.

"No way, man. Val, Dev, and Khep are mortal. If this gets wild like I'm hoping, we'll totally ruin the mood if one of them gets burnt. Khepri can regenerate, but the others can't."

The shithead went from a larva to an adult dung beetle to a full-grown man in less than twelve hours. I was impressed, but also slightly jealous because once he'd switched from bug form to human, Val had cuddled him the entire time in her lap as he grew —*lucky bastard*.

I want to grow on her lap. Or, at least, let certain parts of me grow on her lap.

Raiden grunts, "Well, how do you set the mood?"

"Easy peasy, lemon squeezy," I tell him as we set the cooler down in the burnt dirt.

I had to scorch a good chunk of the meadow after yesterday's fight to clean up. So, now, while our tiny home isn't in the most scenic of spots, at least we aren't staring at zombie cow carcasses all over the place.

It's clean, which was one of Val's prerequisites, and that means it's a go for sexy times.

Genius that I am, I know exactly what we need to do to *tickle her feathers*. I grab a white plastic bag out from beside the hot tub. I unzip it and pull out four adult-male swan costumes.

"Try one on," I command to the uptight former guard.

Raiden's jaw predictably drops.

"You're not serious."

"No waves, no glory," I tell him—*I watched like ten epic surf shows on Netflix my last week in prison and I'm totally rocking the lingo.*

He shakes his head.

"You wanna see that long, curved neck of Val's? You want to trace those tiny black marks on her beak with your tongue?"

He shudders and gets a stiffie, though he tries to hide it with his hand. "That's just Aphrodite's curse."

I stride over and check the temperature on the hot tub I got delivered this morning from a grateful Chubby, who's hiding out somewhere in the stars and whose mother—apparently—is a human who owns a hot tub store. The water's bubbling and it's perfect.

"Your loss," I tell him as I struggle into the pants of my own costume. As a rule, I don't like pants, but this is a special occasion. The pants sag a bit because the tail feathers are pretty heavy, so I tuck them into the seam of my undies, hoping that will help. I leave off the wings for a moment and put on the head next, just like the costume shop attendant recommended. The neck and head of the swan costume are full of foam and I have to put an elastic strap under my chin to hold it on. Even with the strap, the stuffed swan head is about three feet above my own and it wobbles when I move.

"You look ridiculous! Take that off!" Raiden growls, his eyes narrowing to slits.

I just flex my pecs at him and then move side to side. Then I practice nodding my head, like I saw those swans do on that YouTube mating video Dev showed me.

Khepri walks out of our tiny house to see what the disturbance is.

He stops dead at the sight of my epic costume as I pause my mating dance practice to shrug on the wings. I'm supposed to flap them along with the head bobbing.

"What the Duat ..." His face curls up in confusion.

"This idiot thinks we're going to seduce Val with swan costumes." Raiden jabs a very rude finger at me.

I defend myself. "Dude, our lady love transforms into a swan. She deserves to be courted in a way that appeals—" Logic does nothing for the lightning god, who rolls his eyes, so I cut myself off. Why bother with him? He'll regret it when Val sees what I've done.

Khepri comes forward and grabs my remaining costumes.

Hell yeah! Someone knows what's up. I do a 'told you so' head bob in Raiden's direction and wait for Khepri to don the epicness.

But he just holds out a hand. A giant pile of shit ends up on top of the remaining costumes.

"Dammit! Those were rentals!" I yell.

"Don't care," he points an open palm toward me. "Take it off or I'll do the same to you." I glare at him.

Raiden tells Khepri, "Do it anyway. Then the rest of us can have an orgy with Val while he takes a shower by himself." I send a flame his way but he just retaliates with a lightning bolt that jolts my bones and makes my teeth clench.

I glare at him as I begrudgingly strip off the costume. "I'm gonna make sure you're the guy who *just* gets a handy," I threaten Raiden as Khepri hardens the shit on the costumes so it doesn't stink.

"Please, you're the only one she hasn't screwed, think there might be a reason for that?" he grouches.

"Yeah. It's called saving the best for last!" I tell him as I shrug off my wings in a hurry, ready to punch him in his face.

"What's going on out here?" Val and Dev come out the front door hand-in-hand.

Immediately, we all stop fighting and turn to stare.

She's a vision, a miracle, a necromancer who could raise every boner in the graveyard. She's wearing a short purple dress today that makes my entire body pulse with need. I sigh at the sight of her.

"I'd prepared a romantic evening for you, my lady. But these douchebags have ruined it," I report.

"He wanted to have furry-style costume sex in a hot-tub," Raiden debases my intentions.

"No. I wanted to seduce your swan form in the physical language that appeals to those senses." I protest. "We were going to do a dance to seduce you."

I walk over to a cooler and throw it open. I pull out a platter of chocolate covered strawberries. "Then I wanted to seduce your human form with treats and massages and a hot tub. I love you Val. All of you. And I want you to know."

Val drops Dev's hand and comes toward me, lips pressed together in a small smile. Does she like my romantic sentiments? Or will she mock me, too? I don't like to admit, even to myself, how nervous that makes me.

Val runs her hand down my shoulder. "Thank you, Lover." She adds a purr to my chosen nickname and that gives me hope.

I reach out and carefully put the fingers from my free hand on her waist. I want to go further, but I'm not sure this is the right moment.

"Your intentions are always … sweet," she adds. She rises up on her tiptoes and leans toward me.

My pulse starts racing. My palms get sweaty and I worry I'm gonna dump the tray of strawberries right onto her.

She leans in closer and I can see each of her eyelashes, closer and I can see every dimple in her lips, a tiny freckle on one side of her nose. For the first time in my existence, I can't tell exactly what time it is. It feels like time has slowed down. I don't feel tied to the sun. I feel tied to her. Then her lips brush mine and I know that I've just changed forever.

Val kisses me softly, her lips plucking at mine like I'm some instrument and she's a musician. My body vibrates with every touch.

I take the smallest step forward, moving the tray of strawberries to the side so that my chest can touch hers.

The brush of her nipples against my abs sends a wave of pleasure through me. My dick hardens against her stomach. I hear her hum of satisfaction against my mouth and I move closer.

Everyone, everything else is forgotten.

Until I drop the tray of strawberries.

They fall to the ground and bounce along, getting covered in dirt.

"No!" I break from our kiss and stare down at the berries, which now look like tiny shits. I cover my face with my hands. "Everything is ruined. The costumes! The berries!"

"Tupac," Val's hands wrap around my waist, but I can't look at her.

My perfect seduction has been foiled in every way.

"Tupac," Val says louder. Her hand comes up to my chin and turns me to face her.

I stare down into her lovely, stormy blue eyes.

"Yes?" I whisper.

"Asteio called me this morning. He told me you had quite the reputation among the prisoners … for dancing."

I swallow hard as my dick thickens and lengthens. Is she talking about …?

Her eyes travel south.

She is!

I take a step backward and reach for the phone I'd set near the hot tub.

I open the music app and immediately, "Swan Lake" orchestral music starts blaring through the speakers.

Quickly, I type in my search bar to find the song I actually want.

M.C. Hammer's greatest composition of all time pops up.

I strike a pose.

And then I let my dick dance.

VAL

THE GUYS SNICKER BEHIND ME, BUT I'M ENTRANCED.
Tupac's control over his dick is epic. He can pulse it
quickly, slowly, right and left. His ass muscles clench
and he thrusts his pelvis in time with the music, like it's
the base beat and his dick works the lyrics.

Fuck.

Can he do that ... inside of me?

I have to know.

I run forward and jump on top of him, latching my
legs around his back. He falls backward into the dirt,
not expecting my move. But I don't let up. I kiss him
and bite his lower lip as I grind against that incredibly
talented dick.

"Shit, was he right about the mating dance thing?"
Raiden asks behind us.

But I'm too focused on sliding my hand into Lover's
underwear to listen. I make my way underneath that

embroidered sun and wrap my hand around his hot, thick cock.

"Make it pulse again," I order.

Tupac does. His rod taps my pussy through the skirt of my dress repeatedly.

Fuck.

I slide up a little so he's more aligned with my clit. "Again," I tell him.

I feel his grin against my lips as he starts up again. His rhythm is the perfect tease. I start to move against him and I can feel my orgasm building.

But then he does something naughty. Tupac starts moving his dick diagonally, so that he doesn't hit my clit directly.

"Lover, no fair!" I mewl.

"This is supposed to be an orgy, Val," he reminds me gently.

I pull back to study his eyes. "You don't want me first?"

His hand reaches back and squeezes my ass, pulling me into him so his dick can pulse doubletime against my clit.

The answer to my question is lost as my mind becomes a hazy mess.

This time, Lover doesn't tease. He lives up to his nickname. His dick works better than my old vibrator, heating my clit and tapping it with just the right amount of pressure until I grab his shoulders and start to scream.

Tupac uses that opening to lean up and put his lips on my breasts. He kisses one nipple, then laves it roughly through my dress, adding to the sensation and setting off a second, smaller orgasm as my hips jut into his again and again.

"I want you," he mutters. "First and last and always. But … I've been imagining the perfect orgy for nearly four hundred years."

I feel boneless. I want nothing more than to collapse on top of him and have him rub my back gently.

But that's not what Tupac needs. My horny mate needs more. He deserves more. He sat and watched patiently through my first time with Dev. So, instead of collapsing, I put my hands on the ground on either side of him and stare down into his face. I kiss the scruff on his chin. And I ask, "What's your perfect orgy?"

Tupac's eyes get teary as he asks, "Really?"

And with the expression on his face, how could I refuse him anything? After all, the man was willing to dress up in a swan suit to impress me.

"I want to watch you try to stand completely still while Dev eats you out and Khepri licks your nipples."

Just the mental image has me pushing up to my feet. Hell fucking yes. I love Tupac's idea of an orgy. "Did you hear him?"

The question is hardly out of my mouth before a naked Khepri and Dev are on me. Khepri rips off my dress and tosses it on the ground. Dev is much more gentle. He slowly slides my panties down my legs and helps me step out of them. He leaves on my Greek-inspired wrap sandals.

"Oh, Hanan Pacha,[1] you're beautiful," Tupac says.

Dev gently pushes my legs further apart, so that he has room to kneel between them. His head leans forward between my parted thighs and he starts to lick up one thigh and then down the other.

Khepri stands to one side and bends so that his lips can latch onto my nipple. He suckles gently at first, and my hand goes to his black hair, to run over the short, shorn locks.

I look out to see Lover stroking himself and smiling. "Perfect, yes."

Raiden moves toward my free breast; he's the only man still fully dressed, but Lover waves him away. "No, no. It won't work with three. Only two."

I jut out my lower lip and plead with Lover. "Can't he touch me somewhere?" I need all of them to touch me.

Tupac slows his jerking and lets his eyes roam up and down my body as Dev starts to lick me more directly. My entire body tightens up and Khepri notices, latching harder in order to bring me closer to climax.

"Fine," I hear Tupac tell Raiden as I struggle to stay upright, "You lube a finger and tease her ass."

I don't even have the ability to respond because the sky has gone hazy. The trees have disappeared from my vision. I can't see anything beyond Lover gently stroking his dick and watching the others pleasure me. I can't feel anything beyond the heat that's building in my center and shooting up my spine.

Raiden sucks on his index finger as he walks behind me. He gently slides that wet finger up the back of my thigh, over the curve of my ass. He traces the crease just as my vision starts to ripple like a pond.

The hot wet finger traces my back hole and it's the final straw. I explode into rapture. I shake, and three sets of hands surround me to keep me still as two mouths and one finger continue to wring pleasure from my body.

Raiden's finger slips inside just as another wave of pleasure consumes me. I jerk forward and Khepri's teeth nip at my breast. Devin realizes what's happening, but instead of helping hold me in place, he takes a hand off of me and slides his own finger into my pussy. He and Raiden get a rhythm going and I start to moan, throwing my head back on Raiden's shoulder until I'm roughly yanked upright by my hair.

"Stay standing Val," Tupac warns me, his voice dark and commanding in a way I've never heard before. He pulls my head forward and locks me in a kiss.

My legs start to shake. My arms fly up. I lock one around Khepri and the other around Tupac because otherwise I'm going to fall and crush Dev. My legs can't hold me up anymore.

Yet another orgasm courses through me and Lover

swallows my satisfied moans with his mouth as it moves over my lips.

When it's over, I whimper, "I can't. I can't—"

Tupac says, "Dev, Raiden, stand back. She's ready for the main event."

They listen, carefully sliding out of me and backing away. Khepri releases my breast but keeps hold of my arm around his shoulder.

Tupac slowly sinks to the ground, pulling me onto his lap and onto his very hard, thick dick.

As he slides into me, I groan. I'm already boneless. I've had so many orgasms. I don't think I can take any more.

"Yes you can," he tells me, and I realize I've spoken aloud.

I just stare up at his soulful brown eyes. He's been right so far. This orgy has been better than my wildest dreams. So I decide to trust him. I nod.

Tupac reclines back slightly, pulling me so that I'm leaning forward on top of him. "Dev, come fill her ass."

My eyes widen and my mouth pops open to protest. But just then, Lover makes his dick dance. Inside me.

Holy fucking cupid babies, that feels good!

Dev spits and lubricates his dick before gently pushing into me. At first, it's too much. It hurts—but then Lover's dick pulses again, distracting me, teasing me, bringing me to a new high.

And then he and Dev start to move, one sliding farther in as the other slides out. My body becomes the instrument of their pleasure and I slip into a mental and emotional space I've never been before. I feel wild and vulnerable, trapped and free at the same moment.

Tupac gives me some time to get used to their rhythm and then he says, "Val, I need you to swallow Khepri's cum. And I want you to let Raiden cum all over those tits."

I'm past the point of talking. My brain has shut down to base functions. Pleasure and … well pleasure. Because everything's now making hot swirling sensations spread through my lower abdomen. My eyelids flutter and I let my mouth pop open. I lift a hand.

If the other two want me, they're going to have to do the rest. Because I'm maxed out.

I feel the head of Khepri's dick tease my lips. It's already slick with precum. I open wider and let him slip inside.

Seconds later, Raiden's dick slides between my fingertips and I grip him tightly. I hold on and hold still as they work themselves into a frenzy.

It doesn't take long after the foreplay they've just given me.

Khepri comes first, unloading down my throat with a massive groan. I struggle to swallow it all down.

As soon as the scarab god steps back, Raiden takes his place. His dick is hardly between my lips before he pulls back and sprays my chin and then my chest with his cum.

Tupac slides inside me and stops thrusting. Instead

he starts pulsing again, faster and faster until I scream in pleasure. I clench around him and as I do, I feel Dev give my thighs a hard squeeze and his dick unloads into my ass. Seconds later, Tupac follows suit, filling me up.

I collapse on top of Lover, a sweaty, cum-covered mess. I laugh, with my cheek on his chest. "That was the best orgy I've ever been part of."

"You've been part of another?" Dev asks curiously from where he's laid down in the dirt beside us.

"Nope," I tell him.

Beneath me, Tupac chuckles. "That was just round one of the orgy. My fantasy isn't done until we've hit the hot tub, the stairs, Raiden's altar—"

"Hey—" Raiden interjects.

"You can't be serious," I tell him.

But he is. And we don't stop until every one of Tupac's naughty dreams comes true.

"ARE YOU SURE ABOUT THIS?" TUPAC ASKS ME AS WE wait outside of our tiny—albeit gigantic on the inside —house.

I fiddle my thumbs together nervously—a feeling that I *despise*.

"Yes," I say quietly. "I'm sure."

Tupac claps a hand on my back. "You got this, Homeskillet."

I chuckle, not even bothering to ask what this new saying means. Tupac is always quoting humanisms that make no sense. I return gazing at my hands. I meant what I said to the demigod—I *am* sure about this decision. Unfortunately, it and everything else have cost me my entire relationship with my family.

That's right, the honorable—read self-righteous— Izanami and Izanagi, a.k.a my mother and father, decreed me a stain on the old and noble legacy of

Japanese gods. Effectively, they've disowned me and do not consider me part of the pantheon any more—which is fine with me since humans could give two shits about us.

When's the last time you Googled a Shinto god?

A combination of releasing the 'abominations' (a.k.a demigods), and being in a relationship *with* one forced my parents (forced is their word—not mine) to take drastic measures: either be cut off permanently or return to my former glory and forget about Val and my friends. Basically, go back to an eternity of pleasing them in dull servitude.

I chose Val.

Hell, I chose an eternity of *Khepri* over my parents.

It was hard—not my decision, but turning my back on years of duty and, of course, my family. I love my family, but I love Val more. She's like this bright, vibrant, jagged streak of lightning. She's energetic, unpredictable, and completely captivating.

That's why I'm here now, waiting with Tupac. I watch the woods, swirling with mist, and a figure emerges from it, *Thor*, his reddish beard and hair glinting in the sun.

"Raiden-Sama! Tupac! How's my Sigrdrifa?" he booms.

"Val is well, sir," I answer, putting my hands behind my back and standing at attention.

"Yeah, especially with all the s-e—" Tupac starts.

"Ignore him," I direct to Val's dad, cutting off the sex-addled demi.

I swear to the gods that he only thinks with the head in his sun-embroidered banana hammock.

"Thanks for coming. We appreciate this," I tell Thor, who nods.

"And you've talked to Val about this decision?"

I look at Tupac, then turn to answer. "No, sir. We haven't—only because we think she would try to talk us out of it."

"Smart man. Sigrdrifa is the smartest of my children, and the most difficult—don't tell her I said that or I'll send your asses to the Land of Evil Frost Giants."

Tupac laughs, but I don't think the Norse God of Thunder is joking.

"If this is your choice, then here is what you seek," Thor says, pulling a dagger out of thin air.

It's exactly the same as the one Ra wielded—*a death dagger*. Thor had it made for us, by appealing to a wide variety of gods.

"Thank you, sir," I tell him with a bow, taking the weapon into my hands.

It seems odd that something so small will change my fate forever but, often, that's the case. One insignificant item can change a life. One look from a beautiful woman can change a heart. My impending mortality is making me philosophical.

I straighten back up and look to Tupac, who raises a challenging brow at me. In answer, I press the tip of the blade into one of my thumbs. I wait, but don't feel anything to indicate that my immortality is gone.

I raise a hand to the sky and clouds gather at my command. My powers are still intact, but suddenly it hits me. Somehow, I know without a doubt that I'm just as vulnerable as a human.

It's an unsettling feeling.

Tupac takes the death dagger from me and wipes my blood on my kimono. I scowl at the irritating man who thinks about sex way too much—I'm never going to get the red stain out of silk. Tupac smirks, clearly enjoying my ill-concealed ire, and flexes his left arm.

"See these guns? This is why our little swan likes me," he jokes and both Thor and I roll our eyes.

"Would you just prick yourself already?" I snap.

"I've tried," the Aztec demi sighs. "Even my impressive length can't reach my ass—"

I take the dagger from him and dig the tip into his bicep to shut him the fuck up. Tupac hisses is pain and I grin with satisfaction. I don't bother cleaning off Tupac's blood, but hand the dagger back to Thor, who uses some mystifying power to vanish it into thin air.

Just in time, too, because Val comes bounding from the house.

"Dad! What are you doing here?" she asks.

"I've come to talk and see if you're done recovering." He gives us a wink.

I try to wink back, but I've never done it before. Winking was for those with secrets. Secrets were dishonorable, according to my parents. Thus, my attempt at winking becomes more of an awkward set of rapid blinks.

"By recovering, does he mean fu—" Tupac starts and Val rushes to clap a hand over his mouth.

"We're done recovering," she confirms. The way her face flushes in embarrassment has me snickering.

Dev and Khepri come out to shake Thor's hand and we give him the details of our final battle with Ra.

"I'm so proud of you, my daughter," he commends Val.

"Thank you, but it wasn't just me—it was all of us working together as a team."

"I know. They have proven themselves worthy of your love many times over. I hope you will remember this," Thor comments, making Val raise a brow.

"Why would I need to remember *that*?"

"See what I mean? Too smart for her own good," Thor stage-whispers to Tupac and me, and I feel my stomach drop a bit.

"What's going on?" Val demands and I groan.

"Way to throw us under the bus," I mutter to the red-haired menace.

"I've had to clean up a lot of your shit—metaphorically *and* literally speaking. Forgive me if I'm not sorry for your plight," he taunts right back.

I glare at Khepri, who just grins. Any *literal shit* is all *his* fault.

"Well?" Val orders impatiently.

"Raiden asked your dad to get a death dagger to stab ourselves with to strip our immortality so that we could be like you, Khep, and Dev," Tupac says, ratting us both out, but placing the blame on my shoulders.

Val's mouth forms a perfect O of shock and I think about the ways I'm going to kill the solar demi ... I'll start by cutting off his dick, I can promise you that.

But Val surprises us both. She bursts into tears and throws herself into my arms.

"You made yourself mortal to live out the rest of your life with me—and the others?! You sweet, thoughtful, irresistible—"

Val stops mid-sentence to kiss me—*right in front of her dad.*

"What?!" Tupac shrieks. "Why is he getting all the tongue action?!"

Val takes her time before pulling away from me.

"I wasn't using my tongue and you're just jealous," she corrects Tupac. "But, come here."

Val yanks the sun demi to her, but Khepri stops her.

"Do you really want one of your ... ah, boyfriends to get a boner in front of your father?"

"Good point," she whispers, stepping away from Tupac, who looks ready to cry at having missed the chance at Val's lips on his. "Later," she promises him.

Thor looks on in amusement.

"Young love—it's so refreshing," he jokes, making Val giggle and roll her eyes.

"Speaking of *love* ... how's, um, everything back in Asgard?"

Thor raises a sardonic brow. "A pain in the ass, as usual, but you won't have to worry about your step-mothers or siblings *ever* again."

The implacable way he states his words make a shiver run down my spine. The powerful lightning god finally checked his family and I'm grateful on Val's behalf.

"I've also spoken with Aphrodite—she shouldn't be a problem, either, not with that website Dev created that would make her known as the goddess of STDs. As for the other gods, I've rallied the most powerful together to ensure that nothing like this happens ever again. Some gods and goddesses don't agree," he states, pausing to look understandingly at me since my parents are among those 'purist' gods and goddesses, "but those in favor of creating freedom and equal rights for demis are the majority. We will always strive to ensure demigods are safe ... something that should have been done long ago," he finishes sadly.

Val rests a hand on his arm. "Thank you—for everything."

I look away, my heart both swelling in happiness and shattering at the same time. I'm so overjoyed that Val has her father—something I will never have again, but I know I've made the right choice. I've come a long way. And for the first time in my life, I can genuinely say that I'm happy—I even laugh spontaneously, sometimes.

Trust me—*it shocks the others as much as me.*

Val and the guys have taught me how to live and, as cheesy as it sounds, to laugh and love.

"Before I go, I brought back Asteio and the Demigodling for a visit," Thor announces. "I left them in the woods with my goats and chariot."

Val cringes.

"I don't know if that was a good idea ..."

"Yeah, Asteio might try to get frisky with them," Dev jokes and Thor blanches.

"He better fucking not—"

"You know, just because I'm part goat, doesn't mean I screw goats," Asteio sniffs, coming out of the woods with the Demingodling's arm flung across his shoulders.

"Sorry, dude. I didn't mean—" Dev apologizes, but the Demigodling just laughs.

"He's kidding; he's totally into beastiality," The Demigodling pokes a teasing finger at Asteio's chest.

"AH!" Val cries, her hands flying up to cover her ears. "Lalalalala—TMI!"

We all laugh at her antics.

"We've got all the websites updated," the Demigodling tells Dev.

"Awesome—that should help in really destabilizing some of the more powerful gods who are still against demis."

"More than Aphrodite's site? Do I want to know?" Thor asks with an arched brow.

"Ignorance is bliss," Val teases and the mighty thunder god chuckles.

"That's your human side speaking—gods are far too nosy. But, this old man doesn't want—or need—to know anything more. Enjoy your time ... recovering. And, maybe, consider coming home for a family dinner or two from time to time—but leave the Visine behind," he orders sternly.

Val bites her lip to keep from giggling. "Yes, sir," she tells him with a mock salute before she dives in for a hug.

"Call if you need anything, daughter," he orders gruffly—lovingly.

"I will. Bye, Dad."

"Bye, Sigr—I mean, *Val.*"

Thor leaves the same way he came, but Asteio and the Demigodling stay behind. Uncomfortably, I realize that I've spent a lifetime calling this man 'Demigodling.' Awkwardly, I ask him if he has a name.

"Of course, I have a name. It means 'most exalted' in ancient Egyptian."

"Neat!" Val says. "What is it?"

"Khak."

Nobody says anything for a moment, but Tupac's face lights up in a lascivious grin.

"Did someone say cock?" he asks and we all groan.

One thing's for sure—*life with him and the others will never be dull.*

Khepri looks over at me and winks conspiratorially, making me shake my head.

"Well, best friend," he jokes, "it's good to know I'm not the most annoying one in the group."

I harrumph in mock exasperation. "Yes, you are," I return. "Why do you think I gave up my immortality? Because I didn't want to spend eternity putting up with your shit!"

Val hears this and her laughter rings out around us joyously.

"The shit jokes are never going to stop, are they?" Khepri laments.

"Not until death do us part," Dev teases, but Val sucks in a breath.

"I do," she whispers to him tenderly, making the rest of us look on in confusion.

"What just happened?" Tupac whispers to me.

"Dude, I think they just got married—which means your turn is coming," Asteio answers. "The good news, I've got an unlimited supply of booze for the reception!"

"Party, party, party!" Khak begins to chant ...

And that's how all the demigodlings came to have a wild, booze-filled, *completely* consensual, magical, shape-shifted, bestiality-style orgy at our house—but, that's a story for another day.

ACKNOWLEDGMENTS

Thank you to our husbands.

Thanks to our kiddos for reinvigorating our sense of potty humor.

Thanks to Kimberly Snagg at KDS Cover Concepts for the awesome cover.

Thanks to our amazing ARC readers and betas, specifically: Kelly, Mandi, Shanti, and Thais.

ABOUT THE AUTHORS

MJ is totally more hip and cool than Ann. As in hippie.
She likes to tend to her herb garden and play sequence
and nap, as though she's eighty on the inside.

Ann, however, knows what's up. She's the mom with
no makeup and a tangled ponytail in the pick up line at
school, back when there was school. Now ... she just
chases kids around the house and wonders that she has
any hair left. Most of it has been pulled out in frustration.

Both women have extensive potty mouths in their
books, but ironically, not so much in real life.

But, if you loved our foul mouthed humor in this book,
you might like ...

Magical Academy for Delinquents (Pinnacle Book 1)

Knightfall (Tangled Crowns Book 1)

NOTES

PRELUDE

1. History time! Ra (the insecure prick) feared Nut and Geb's children would be a threat. As god of the skies and time, Ra decreed Nut couldn't give birth on any day of the year to keep her pregnant and suffering heartburn for eternity.

   But Nut went to Thoth, god of wisdom, for help and he made a bet with Khonsu, god of the moon.

   Thoth whipped moon-boy's ass and took light as payment. He used it to make five days not part of the year. From then on, the moon was never as bright as the sun, and Nut was finally able to give birth. She had five children: Osirus, Horus, Set, Isis, and Nephthys.

2. Remember how Ra was fucking furious and separated Nut from Geb for eternity?

   Nut was banished to the stars, but when Ra had to push the sun through Duat, the underworld (because Khepri fucking quit), Nut searched the Earth for her beloved.

   She never did find Geb. Instead, Nut found a humble human. They fell in love and Nut once more became pregnant. This time, she went into the underworld, where Ra's authority is limited. She gave birth to her demigod there and proclaimed him the true king of Egypt.

   The humans embraced him. Everyone bowed down and the child god was made into the pharaoh.

   Ra, also known as god of kings, was livid. Not only did the people worship this half-human more than him, they also took his divine right away to make this brat a king. Moral: It sucks to be Ra. It also sucks to piss Ra off. Hence, our story.

1. VAL

1. Real wind. Not 'breaking wind.'
2. Australian god of wet panties.
3. A Valkyrie whose name means 'wearing a war ax,' also synonymous with *skank*.
4. The name of Thor's infamous hammer—the actual tool, not his dick. Get your mind out of the gutter.
5. Cod's tongue—it's a fucking delicacy, I swear.

2. DEV

1. Aeneus is a Trojan prince, son of Greek goddess Aphrodite and the human prince Anchises. He was involved in the Trojan War which, unfortunately, was not a war over condoms.
2. Forgive Dev's ignorance here. Modern people/characters don't know that Cupid/Eros are the same person and history has lots of conflated stories of winged babies flying around shooting people up with love hormones. These stories don't make sense, because babies should serve as hormone killers, warnings, etc. But myths are what they are.

5. VAL

1. King of heaven, per our thorough research on Wikipedia.
2. We were really hoping there would be a Tiandong. But, alas, gong is as close as it gets. We'll just have to pretend the duke of heaven is named dong.
3. For people who haven't seen the hottest of the Avengers superhero movies, Loki is Thor's brother.' But not really. But ... it's complicated and not really relevant to this particular story so we'll leave it at that and let you go drool over Chris Hemsworth if you really want to know more about Loki. (And yes, we know that's not the most historically accurate place to send you for info on Norse mythology. But it's the hottest. So ... priorities.)
4. Idunn is the Norse goddess of youth who grows apples that

keep the gods young. Her name is not "eye-dun" but "yo-dune" kind of like Yoda, except she's not green, so far as we know.

6. KHEPRI

1. The Egyptian city known as the 'City of the Sun God' where Ra wanked off to his golden statues among the worshipping humans.

8. THE ORIGINAL TUPAC

1. Inti is Quechua for *sun*. I can think of nothing snarky to say about that this morning as I'm not fully caffeinated. Thanks for reading the footnote anyway.
2. A pastime some people like where they weave patterns and shit out of cloth.
3. Zulu goddess of rainbow, harvests, rain, and beer. So basically everything good. She also has a kickass story so we're putting it here. She couldn't find a hubby amongst the gods, so she found an earthly lover. But, to test his love, she disguised herself as a hag and sent a beautiful woman his way. Her lover immediately recognized her—*ignoring Big Boobs McGee*—and they were married that day. They now live in a rainbow house in the sky —*awwww*.
4. Incans could have multiple wives, depending on their ability to work. Women and men often had trial marriages to ensure they were compatible. (Can we give a quick shoutout to a culture that didn't value virginity as the sign of a woman's worth?) If a man's labor was able to support multiple wives (a sign of prestige) then he could take on secondary wives. But his primary wife would be in charge, bitches.

10. RAIDEN

1. Shinto hell. Try telling someone to go to Yomi. Let me know how it goes.
2. Haitian Voodoo god of harvest, not necessarily known for Jello, but it deserves a god, don't you think?

11. VAL

1. Valkyrie of protection, mercy, patience that could choose to heal the dead. A really pointless exercise in futility since her sisters would just kill the person again.

12. DEV

1. Gaelic god of wild beasts about whom nearly nothing is known so academics just make shit up.
2. This is just one example of Poseidon's asshole tendencies. Greek gods were general assaultist dicks.
3. Tala is the eldest daughter of Phillipino sun god Arao, who was tricked into devouring some of his children by the moon goddess (since she was afraid his children would "eclipse" hers. He, understandably, got a bit bitter about it.
4. If you feel like a-Googling, check out the pics of Chinnamasta.

14. KHEPRI

1. Thor's dad is Odin, the top dog Norse god. He also has only one eye—which he exchanged to become more divine—making Val very punny.

15. VAL

1. The Norse world of mist, but also where Hel resided. Basically, saying 'what in the hell.'
2. Ve is the brother of Odin, who's historically gotten all the Norse glory. His name and the fact that he supposedly *created* humans has passed down, but nothing else. Bummer for him that we thank the god of wisdom and death more than the creator.
3. Land of the Light Elves—you know, the good ones from LOTR.

16. TUPAC

1. Apollo's musical battle against Pan is legendary: lyre versus Pan's pipes. Think of the epic rap battles Biggie and the second Tupac and you'll get the idea. Apollo gave King Midas the ears of an ass for voting against him. He gave them to Khepri too, but obviously, Khepri was removed from all retellings because those greedy Greek gods don't want to share their legends with other deities.
2. Originally, unicorns were described by the Greeks as having the tail of a lion and hooves of a boar. Slightly different from the pretty horsies with a horn shoved on their head that we describe today.
3. Roman goddess who protects against fires. She was actually super important back in the day,when fires could decimate entire cities.

18. RAIDEN

1. Shinto word for soul, not a braless tank top.

19. VAL

1. Rhymes with the English word 'pen', which is ironically the
   word for a female swan. Khen is not to be confused with
   Barbie's bitch lover.

22. KHEPRI

1. This style of fighting is old and peppered throughout Egyptian
   history. It was used to settle scores, keep our bodies fit, and to
   entertain the masses.
2. Supposedly, the fakest wrestler in the WWE, according to one
   website whose veracity is questionable.

25. VAL

1. Incan heaven